MW00933760

# Why Won't She Call Me Back?

*a Ray Brautigan Mystery*

*by Joe Rice*

*For Roger, the best bartender I ever had*

# CHAPTER ONE

*'Christ, I can't do this anymore,'* Ray thought. His head felt like it was trying to spontaneously develop telepathy. Or telekinesis. Whatever would make it hurt like fuck. His stomach had that "I'm going to squirt hot liquid out your ass all day so get used to it," feeling. His mouth felt coated with chap-stick and sand and it tasted like failure.

He checked the clock and it was three. P.M., he was pretty sure. He had an appointment at six and it wasn't too far away.

His apartment had, depending on how you looked at it, two or three rooms. There was his bathroom, where the toilet touched the shower and the sink gave up on working when people were deciding whether or not to vote for Dukakis. There was also a room with a dirty futon and interesting smells and piles of debris. The "third" room was the "closet" that held his building's water-heater. It was hot and it was loud, but it got Ray a little discount on the rent.

Ray grabbed the cheap jug of bourbon and drank some breakfast. "Fuck you, you piece of shit," he said to his stomach. He gave his liver the bird. The bourbon tasted as cheap as it was, but after a fourth big slug, he stopped giving a damn.

Booze had long lost its fun—back in college he drank because he didn't want to be an accountant. When he quit that and followed his photography dream, he drank because he was happy and that's what artists do. That all fell to shit, of course, and now he just drank.

Ray counted the bags under his eyes in the mirror. His thick glasses kind of hid them to the public, but Ray could hear those bags say "Get better sleep, you dick." His hair was shit-brown and without any discernable style. He was thin, maybe even skinny, except for a burgeoning pot-belly . . .the physique of the poorly-nourished. Looking at himself naked filled him with self-hate, so he took another drink.

He showered in a haze, almost used to the wildly fluctuating water temperature. He wiped his body hair out of the tub and filled it and the broken sink with some watered-down photo chemicals and went to work on the Mrs. Higgins pictures. Specifically, he was developing and printing the ones of her fucking the security guard from her local bank. Mr. Higgins would be waiting at six and the photos had to be clear enough to be conclusive, but not quite "Hustler." Nobody wants to see someone else's jizz on their wife's tits. Well, some people do, but probably not Mr. Higgins. Just didn't seem the type.

He printed up a few choice photos and hung them out to dry. Went in to go sit on the futon and smoke the rest of a cigarette he had started the night before. Today was . . .Tuesday? No, Wednesday. After savoring the smoke as slowly as a woman takes a piss, Ray gathered up the mostly-dry photos into a file and left his apartment. It was hot, of course. Vegas always was.

He dropped by a hot dog joint for some cheap solid breakfast to help hold the bourbon down. Eating them on the way made the walk to the meeting seem shorter, anyway. When the economy was booming, he hadn't needed to buy a car. There was always someone willing to drive the (then) up-and-coming photographer wherever he needed to go. Once that all went to shit, so did Ray's transportation options.

The Higgins appointment was across town, in one of the hundreds of dives that littered Vegas like houses would a real city. Ray never met clients at a bar he actually frequented. Didn't like mixing his life with the shit he had to do for money. Las Vegas was not a pedestrian-friendly town in most cases, but the stink from Ray's sweat wasn't any worse than the other patrons.

Higgins was late, so Ray had a beer and watched the bar TV. Local news fucks blathered on about stupid shit. Somebody won something, somebody lost something, and poor people killed each other.

Higgins walked in, wearing a stupid jumpsuit with "Higgins Lazer Fun Arcade" embroidered poorly on the back. He stunk of oil and gin—as lovely a combination as you're to find in this world. "Hello, Mr. Higgins. Take a seat," Ray said, though his client was doing so already.

"Cut the shit, Brautigan. You got anything for me?" Higgins was a real master of the long-lost art of conversation.

Ray tossed the file with the photos to him. Higgins slowly opened it and looked carefully at each of the photos. "Goddam whore," he said, staring. "Rotting stinking goddam whore."

They sat there for a moment and Ray glanced at his watch. His friend Ogami had a baseball game that night. First pitch was about to be thrown. "Uh, sir, about my fee . . ." This was always the worst part. When do you ask? How do you ask?

Ray clearly still didn't know the answer to either question. Higgins looked up from the photos for the first time, eyes wet and hot.

"You want your goddam rotten stinking fucking money, you worthless scumshit?" Higgins stood up and dropped a large bag of quarters on Ray's crotch. Two hundred bucks in quarters.

'Don't throw up, don't throw up, don't throw up,' Ray repeated to himself. Something wasn't listening to Ray's brain, though. He threw up promptly while Higgins left the bar.

The bartender, a short ugly woman, sighed. "Get the fuck out of here, asshole."

Ray pulled himself up. He thought about explaining himself but realized it was futile. Nobody gave a shit why this particular drunk was puking up bourbon and hot dogs. Wasn't the type of bar where you told sob stories. He grabbed the bag and limped out. He made it to the closest bus stop and waited to be taken to Ogami's game.

Ogami Burroughs was one of Ray's best friends. Hell, only friends. They met as kids who shared a passion for elaborate GI Joe battles. O went to UNLV on a baseball scholarship and his Japanese mother pressured him into a respectable business major. O hated it as much as Ray did. In fact, O hated most things other than baseball, rock and roll, booze, and women. He partook of all these in great enthusiasm. He played for a minor league ball team, the Vegas Rollers, and fronted a rock band, the Lone Wolves.

On the bus, Ray pulled out his crappy little cell phone. There weren't many contacts. Ogami. Frankie, the guy who sometimes bought his "extra" photos. His mom. And Jenny. Ray met Jenny in art school and she was the only person as close to him as Ogami. When he had first met her, he was, of course, interested in her. She was a petite punk rock spitfire, cuter than ten Mexican babies.

But she was too cool a friend to ever fuck things up by getting naked (Ray often told himself), so that dropped quickly. They became drinking buddies, photography buddies, making fun of retarded people buddies . . . basically, she had been seamlessly inserted into the rest of his life.

She was still getting photography work, and so she'd be out of contact, sometimes for a month at a time. It had been a couple of months since they'd last hung out, so Ray gave her a call.

After the requisite number of rings, he got that same message. "Hey, it's Jenny. Can't make it to the phone right now, so leave me your name, your number, and a mean joke at the beep. Thanks!"

"Uh, hey, it's Ray." Ray hated answering machines like roaches hate it when you turn on the lights. "Uh, going to O's game and then we're probably all going out. Haven't seen you for a while, so, uh, you should come. Call me or something." He hung up and looked at his phone disgustedly.

"Rollers stadium," the bus driver called over the loudspeaker. Ray got out and paid for his ticket in quarters. The girl behind the counter probably cursed at him, but he couldn't hear well through the glass.

Inside, Ray looked around for a place to sit. "Ray! Hello, Ray!" he heard in a thick Brazilian accent. Sophia was O's girlfriend for going on a year now. She was an honest-to-God trapeze girl, the kind that had made Ray's crotch feel funny as a kid at the circus. She worked for this greaseball who was trying to "family up" his shitty casino.

Ray walked over to her and she greeted him with a kiss on each cheek. That always made him feel weird.

"Oh, Ray, you look like shit!" she said. "Oh, I do not mean that in a bitch way. Is everything fine? What happened?"

"Pissed off client," Ray replied, not wanting to go further.

"Who could be pissed off with Ray Brautigan?" she said. Her accent made it difficult to tell when she was teasing. "He is too cute and harmless for anger!"

"How's the game?" Ray asked.

"O struck out and got a single base hit," she said. "He's not zoning yet." Sophia was the first girl Ogami had stayed with for longer than a month, and only the third that lasted more than a weekend. They met at a tattoo parlor and she didn't recognize him from his band or his team. That was a big selling point at the time. She was tall, almost six feet, and had pretty, angular features. Current hair color of choice was a simple jet black. Her AC/DC T-shirt was well-worn and faded. Intricate inkwork nearly covered her left arm. She was tough as hell and nobody tended to piss her off twice. She'd have long ago been resigned to "just one of the boys" status if she weren't so damn pretty.

At Ogami's next at-bat, she called out, "Knock this one very hard!" and whistled shrilly. Ogami doffed his helmet to her with a flourish and put it back on. He wasn't a body builder, but his arms were as big as they were tattooed. He was always an odd presence on the field—unkempt hair, stubble, and that rock and roll swagger. This gave him a mixed relationship with the fans, who either saw him as a deviant, show-boating half-breed or a charismatic star-in-training. In other words, the teenage girls loved him and everyone else hated his half-Jap ass.

The first pitch was a ball but Ogami knocked the shit out of the second and hustled it into a triple. That was the kind of player he was. He took his cues from one Peter Edward Rose. Any time he played, he gave it all he had. Soph and Ray (and the teenage girls) whistled and cheered like crazy.

Soon, the bases were loaded with Ogami getting real itchy on third. The left-fielder, Robinson, was up and he was a strong hitter. He took a stroke, watched a ball, and connected with the third pitch. What happened next is still up for debate. Suffice to say, Ogami charged home and disagreed rather vehemently with the ump's call of "out." In fact, he left forth a string of vulgarity that turned the whole park blue. He was about to throw a punch when he was "escorted" out.

Ray gave Soph a look as they prepared to leave another game early. It had been five whole games since Ogami was last thrown out. This was progress.

# CHAPTER TWO

Later, at the Hole in the Wall Bar, Ogami was still fuming. "Goddam cracker gaijin fuck face shit! I beat that fucking throw by a horse-shitting mile!"

Ray was pretty well toasted by this point. "Fucking asshole!" he blurted. Everyone came to a dead stop. Ogami was the first to laugh. "What?" Ray demanded.

"You're just really funny when you're drunk and angry."

"I should do stand-up then, 'cause I'm always both."

"Hey," Ogami said, "where's Jenny?" Soph elbowed him (too) subtly.

"I dunno. You know Jenny. Maybe I should call her." Ray got up and walked towards the exit. The Hole in the Wall Bar was another dive, yeah, but it was **their** dive. The wallpaper was made up of old 40s and 50s girly photos and the juke had a good variety, from Cash to Nashville Pussy. It was also nice and loud, so Ray stepped outside. He lit a cigarette and thought for a moment.

It had actually been three months since Jenny had even returned his call. Sure, she got busy from time to time, but this was a little ridiculous. Ray feared that she'd just gotten tired of him, or that he'd pissed her off while drunk one night, but he really couldn't remember a damn thing he'd done that was wronger than usual.

He redialed her number and got the same message. "Hey, it's Jenny. Can't make it to the phone right now, so leave me your name, your number, and a mean joke at the beep. Thanks!"

Ray exhaled his cigarette puff and waited for the beep. "Ray again. We're at the Hole. It was a pretty good game, but O got thrown out again. Listen, I haven't heard from you at all in a while. Gimme a call and tell me you're not dead or something. OK, take care, bye."

Ray walked back into the bar and ordered another beer. A large black man in a stylized "Indian" costume entered the bar with a few more traditionally clothed companions. "Chief Black Ass, ladies and gentlemen," one announced. The bar noise died down.

"Chief Black Ass big winner tonight," the big man said. "This round on me!" Cheers from the bar. Vegas doesn't give a shit as long as you're paying.

"Ray?" Ogami poked him. "You're staring."

"It's OK with me," Ray said with a shrug and picked up his beer. Ray next felt himself drinking back in his booth. Ogami was there and then he wasn't. The mix of people kept changing. Was Chief Black Ass with them? Was there singing involved?

Ray saw O kiss Soph. Ray decided to leave. A taxi seemed to magically appear around him, like those motorcycles in *Tron*. Someone told the driver Ray's address. A retarded old man with a dog stared in the car window. Ray either smiled or gave him the finger.

The next thing Ray saw was a pile of photo magazines and skin rags beside his futon. Someone was playing salsa music outside. Again.

Ray sat up stiffly and tried to stretch his back out. He had to sell his bed for food money before he had become a private investigator. This futon wasn't cutting it, but he couldn't afford anything else.

Ray was hungry. The kind of hungry you get after a bender, the dangerous kind. He looked around and found an old bag of corn chips and made a breakfast of them. Cloudy tap water washed it down. He got up and thought that it might be time to jack off again when his mind seemed to fly up past his apartment and his stomach sank downstairs. He ran to the sink, but didn't quite make it and some of his puke splattered on his dirty floor.

"Fuck," he said simply. He got some paper towels and bent down to wipe up his mess. Something was stuck under the broken oven. He pulled and it partially ripped out. A picture of him with Jenny, making stupid faces with arms all jerky. Back when things were fun.

He heard something that sounded like a continued fart. It was barely audible over the salsa outside his window. Farting rats? Did he have farting rats now? No, it was his phone vibrating. He raced over to where he'd left his pants and jerked the phone out.

"Hello?" he said roughly.

"Ray, my boy! It is Frankie!" Christ. Even the fat man's voice made Ray feel like shit. But he was short on cash and couldn't hang up just yet. "How are you doing, my boy? Keeping the pecker clean?"

"Yeah, it's pretty clean," Ray said.

"That is great, you always had some fine tail around with you." Ray didn't bother explaining that the "tail" was always a friend or a girlfriend of a friend or both. "Anyways, I am not calling you to talk about your pecker."

"I figured. Not much to talk about," Ray was tired of the joke.

"Haw! 'Not much to talk about.' You always had a good sense a humor, Ray. Anyways, I need some hot pics."

Ray walked over to his file he kept of photos that he thought Frankie might use. Obscured faces, down and out folks that would never see the pictures, and other worthless scum he dealt with. Ray had almost stopped feeling bad about this side job. "I got the file here. What do you need, Frankie?"

"Niggers, Ray, I need niggers. You will never guess why." Ray never wanted to guess why, but he always was told. "Fucking Klan is coming to town and half those guys can't get enough good shots of niggers. I am talking black chicks, black guys, and especially black guys with white girls or white guys. My boy, those hick motherfuckers must just sit around and circle-jerk to this shit!"

It was like everything that ever came out of Frankie's mouth made the world a worse place to live in. Ray stifled a sigh and looked through the file. "Yeah, I've got some stuff, I guess."

"Big money, Ray. Tall fucking cash. We are talking a hundred bucks a snap, maybe more."

In brighter days, Ray's gallery work sold for thousands. But in these days, this was indeed tall fucking cash. "Shit," Ray said.

"Shit is right, son! Bring everything you have got to Melanie's tonight, ten-ish. Keep fucking them bitches!" That was Frankie's signature goodbye. It always puzzled Ray that no one had stopped him from using it in his fifty odd years of life. He couldn't imagine getting away with that. But Ray wasn't a cheapie crook of indeterminate ethnic background, either. It came with the territory, it would seem.

Ray spent the next hour or two going through all his negatives, looking for anything with a hint of a dark skin tone. With enough of these he could afford a new bed and maybe even a hooker to fuck on said new bed. This got him a little horny, so he put the photos aside and pulled out a porno mag from under the futon. Who he was hiding it from is anyone's guess.

He started stroking it while re-reading the letter about the demanding office lady, but was having trouble staying hard long enough to get anything done. After a half hour or so — he couldn't tell, really — not much was happening.

His phone rang again but he kept at it. A second ring and he was getting closer. Nobody would call him anyway, except Frankie or Jenny. *'Jenny!'* he thought, suddenly ejaculating all over himself. "Fuck!" He leapt up towards his phone, but his jockey shorts tripped him up and he fell flat on his face. "Fuck!" he screamed as he scrambled and picked up his cell. "Hello?" he said, way too loudly.

"Uh, is this, uh, Ray Brautigan?"

It was a female voice. "Speaking, yeah."

"The, uh, private dick?" the voice said with a giggle. That joke never got old. Really.

"Yes, what do you need?" Ray impatiently looked at ejaculate-smeared legs.

"Um, well, I think I need to hire you. I think my, uh, my boyfriend is cheating on me."

*'Then he probably is,'* Ray thought. "And you'd like me to find out for sure," he actually said, groping around for something to wipe himself. "Let's set up an appointment." He wanted this conversation to end quickly.

"When can I come to your office?" she asked. Ray realized he didn't know her name.

"Uh, actually, my office is, uh, undergoing renovations right now. Can we meet at a neutral place, Ms., uh . . ."

"Gordon. You can call me Amy, though. Do you know where Cheers is?" she asked.

"Uh, the one on East Harmon near the school?" '*Fuck*,' he thought. '*College girl. She's going to flake.*'

"Yeah. Can you meet me there at five?" Ray looked at his watch.

"Yeah. What do you look like?"

"I've got brown hair and it's curly. I'll be the girl that looks like she thinks her boyfriend is cheating on her. What do **you** look like?"

"Brown hair, brown eyes, glasses. I'm completely unremarkable. You wouldn't be able to describe me even if you'd met me," Ray's jizz was already drying on his legs.

"Damn, you sounded cute," Ray thought he heard her say.

"What?" he asked, dazed.

"See you then!" she said and hung up.

# CHAPTER THREE

The shower still smelled of chemicals so he rushed through bathing and cut himself three times while shaving. He carefully took the only suit he had left out of the makeshift suit bag he'd made out of the sack that once held his futon mattress. This was his "meeting a new client" suit. It was fashionable back when he was fashionable, but, like on its owner, the wear was definitely showing.

Still, it was the best he had, so he put it on and headed out the door. He immediately started sweating and wished he could afford better deodorant. Or some cologne. Or a car. Or any of the things that normal people do to make themselves impressive or at least presentable.

Cheers was actually within walking distance. He had only been there once and was chased out with a bottle for insisting that Eddie Van Halen was a better guitarist than Stevie Ray Vaughn. Ogami, of course, was with him. He remembered wondering how the most famous bar license in the world would let such an utter shithole carry its name.

As he approached the door, suit stuck to him and wet, he had a momentary panic that they'd recognize him. But Ray had a pretty good eye for faces and he couldn't remember what anyone looked like that night so he calmed down and walked in the door.

He looked around and saw the usual assortment of ugly losers, compulsive gamblers, and dying alcoholics. And a pretty white girl with wavy brown hair, big eyes and cute lips. She was drinking something brown.

She looked up at Ray and made hesitant eye contact that said, "Is that you?" Ray nodded to her silent question and walked over. "Mr.

Brautigan?" she asked. She was wearing a yellow T-shirt that clung tightly to her. Ray tried not to look.

"Yeah, that's me." He was about to pull out the stool next to her but she interrupted him.

"Let's go to a booth. I want this to be private."

"Private dick, that's me." Not as smoothly as he'd hoped.

"We'll see," Amy said, leading him to the back of the bar.

They sat down across from each other and Ray did his best not to look at her tits. So he looked at her drink, which he saw was almost empty. "Uh, can I get you another, uh . . ."

"Scotch," she said. "Thank you very much. Feel free to join me." Ray knew he was in no financial shape to be buying rounds of scotch, but he was self-aware enough to also know he wouldn't be telling her "No" any time soon.

When he returned with the drinks, Amy began her story. It was the same shit as all his other clients, really. Only difference was that she wasn't physically repulsive. Or repulsive at all. Ray's feelings towards the scum that hired him usually varied between "actively wishing them harm" and "actively wishing they'd leave."

Her boyfriend, one Tom Fitzgerald, had been out late a lot, had lost interest in sex. Amy had talked about this part quite a bit, though Ray couldn't tell if it was because she liked talking about sex or the scotch was flowing through her. They apparently had gone from "fucking each other's brains out every night" to "quiet lovemaking when he wasn't too tired."

"I don't want someone to make love to me," Amy said. "I want to fuck. Making love is for pussies."

"Yeah," Ray agreed dumbly. He looked at empty glass in front of him. "Uh, I'm gonna get a beer. You, uh, want something?"

Amy downed the rest of her scotch and nodded. This would be her third in an hour or so. Ray found himself impressed by how the petite girl could hold her liquor.

"So, what do you do, just follow him around?" Amy asked.

The answer was really "Yes" but Ray said, "I've got a process."

"Right," she said, sipping her scotch. "A process. I didn't know guys like you actually existed. 'Private investigator.' Is there, like, a college major for that?"

"Not one that I know of. I was a photographer."

"Really? Are you a pervert? You do this because you like taking pictures of people?" There was a smile in her voice, but he couldn't read the intent. He felt himself get hot and red.

"No! No. I just, well, I'm not good at very much. My friend O's dad used to dick around for an insurance company, and he suggested that if I can't do anything else, I should try this."

"Not good at anything else, uh? That's a shame."

*'Oh, God,'* Ray thought. *'Is she drunk?'*

"Well, hopefully, you'll figure out why I'm not getting laid like I used to. Here," she gave Ray an envelope. "Here's our address, the video store he works at, and a recent picture of us. What do you charge, like, a hundred dollars a day?"

Ray had been paid less before. "Um, yeah. Yeah."

"Plus expenses, whatever that is?"

"It won't be much. I've learned to be, uh, frugal."

"That's fascinating, Ray, it really is. But I gotta get to work. Call me in a day or two with an update."

"Yeah, OK," Ray said. She stood up.

"You gonna walk me out or what?" she asked. Ray scrambled up awkwardly and nodded what he hoped didn't seem like an eager nod. They walked out of the bar together and she pulled two Camel Filters out of a pack and offered him one. Ray hadn't smoked a real brand of cigarettes in months. He took it and was surprised when she lit him.

"Look, I talk a lot of shit," she said, "but at one point I think I loved this guy. I just want to find out if I need to bother anymore. And get laid. I want to get laid more."

"I'll, uh, see what I can do," Ray said, exhaling. He thought that it might have even seemed as cool as he wanted it to.

She gave him a smile, a real smile, and Ray felt his stomach actually flip. "Stay in touch, cutie," she said. Ray watched her walk away and didn't even try to stop himself from staring at her ass.

Eventually, he looked down at his watch. Seven thirty. An hour and a half to eat, get to Fulton Street, and steel himself with enough drink to be able to take Frankie in person. The Big Top was about halfway there and they served free hamburgers during at the bar during "happy hour." And if Soph was working he could probably even get some drinks on the house.

On the bus, Ray thought he felt his phone ringing, but it was just one of those "phantom vibrates." He loosened his tie and pretended not to hear the teenagers in the back of the bus make fun of "whitey."

The Big Top was kind of like everything that had ever been awful about Vegas put together in one place. The owner was most certainly some low level mafia asshole, the kind of guy who jerks off to the Godfather II. It stank like Sinatra and Dino's corpses were in the air vents, even though those guys would've never touched a cheapie shithole like this. And now it was this brightly-painted, commercialized "family-friendly" tourist attraction where local performance artists were paid (usually illegally) to perform like dancing bears.

Ray had known a lot of these people from when they were all doing what they actually liked. But the wheels of commerce had long crunched them up into economic road kill. Soph seemed to enjoy it, though. I guess it helped that she was, in a way, still fulfilling her dream. Trapeze in front of idiot tourists in one place isn't much different than trapeze in front of idiot locals all over the place.

The owner must have gotten some kind of deal on the real estate. The place was pretty damn big for a fourth-rate casino. Big enough for there to be performance areas where Soph and her friends could flip around and do cool shit and not ever be in danger of falling on a paying sap. The red and yellow polka-dot paint scheme was supposed to say "circus" but rarely said much more than a mumbled "migraine."

When Ray walked up to the bar past a few sad clowns, he saw a rare bit of luck. Steve was tending bar. Steve wasn't very interesting, good looking, or really noteworthy at all except for one factor: he had the best buyback policy at the Big Top. Every third drink was free, completely reliably.

"Hey, Steve," Ray said. "Burger and a beer, please." Steve started frying a patty of a quality usually reserved for inner city school children and slid Ray a beer. "Soph on tonight?"

Steve shook his head. "She got the night off," he said needlessly.

Ray couldn't think of anything else to say but, "Oh." He decided to concentrate on his beer and his thoughts, instead.

With Frankie buying all those old photos and Amy paying him a hundred bucks a day, Ray was finally going to have some actual money again. Ray thought excitedly about what he could spend it on. Some better bourbon, to be sure. A bed. Maybe some new clothes or something. Ray thought that he could even take his friends out for a nice dinner. He thought about how nice it would be to have everyone dressed up and eating real food. Jenny, Ogami, Soph ...everyone always looked so good when they dressed up.

The burger was ready and it tasted as good as it had looked. It was food, though, and something truly enjoyable was almost within reach, once Ray got this money.

A mime on a unicycle rode by, juggling something indeterminate. Ray ordered another beer, the third free one already on his mind. Soon enough, it was in his hand.

He almost shivered with disgust, realizing he'd have to meet Frankie soon. At that nasty strip joint, too. Frankie turned his thoughts to his new client and that smile of hers and the way that T-shirt fit her. She was sweet, and funny, and tough as hell. She kind of reminded him of Jenny, but that comparison felt wrong.

Still, she might have even been flirting with him. Ray could never figure out when girls were flirting with him. Back when it still happened, it was kind of funny. These days, it was just safe to assume they weren't. There was also the matter of her being a client, and probably some recently-if-at-all-graduated college kid.

None of that changed her smile, though.

It was time to leave, much as Ray wanted to go for a second trio of beers. The night air was slightly chilled and made the sweat on his back feel terrible. He wanted to take off his suit jacket, but didn't want everyone to see the huge sweat stain so he just walked briskly.

# CHAPTER FOUR

Neighborhoods in Vegas were pretty economically segregated, so Ray often didn't have to walk too far to get from one terrible place to another. Melanie's was just a few blocks away. Ray had never felt very comfortable in strip joints. The truth was, he didn't like being just another creepy guy looking at uninterested naked women. And the women were not really all that attractive even in the dimmest of lighting, especially when compared to the girls he hung out with usually.

Melanie's was even worse. The amount of time Frankie spent there was a clear enough indicator. The girls put up with his shit because he scored them cheap blow and his occasional photo shoots paid fairly well. His leering and groping weren't as bad as some of the drunk tourists that hopped in looking to blow off steam away from the big money clubs.

Ray took a deep breath when he saw the sign. The bouncer asked him for five dollars, but Ray just said, "I'm here for Frankie," and he was let in. The music was as loud as it was bad, and it was total shit. It would have hurt Ray's ears if he weren't used to O's shows.

He saw Frankie in a corner booth with two girls stoned as fuck. Frankie's face was pock-marked from years of squeezing pimples obsessively. He wore a purple silk shirt that would have looked stupid ten years ago when he bought it. Gray chest hair sprung forth from his open collar. He had rings on every finger and the pinky nail on his left hand was long.

"Ray!" he called out, too loud. "Ray! Over here! Over here with these two fine pieces of ass!" If the club had decent lighting, everyone would have seen Ray blush with embarrassment and anger. He shuffled over to Frankie.

"Ray, my friend, my boy, sit down with us. Sit down with Frankie and his friends." Ray was a bit better looking than Frankie, but the girls didn't show any interest in either one. "This is Anastasia. Look at her tits! I bet you would like them in your face!"

"Uh, hi," Ray said. Anastasia said nothing. This was torture. "I brought the photos. You want to see them?"

"Ray, you are too much about the business! Enjoy the tits! Enjoy the pussy! I bet you want these girls to fuck your cock!" Frankie would have lost that bet. "Anastasia, dance on my boy Ray's lap. Give him the extra good dance!"

Anastasia sighed.

"You give him the dance if you want any more shit for your goddam nose!" Saliva exploded out of the fat man's mouth.

Anastasia walked over to Ray and roughly pulled his legs out far enough that she could straddle him on the booth.

"Uh, you don't have to—" Ray started.

"Shut up, faggot," Anastasia replied, taking off her bikini-top. She shoved her tits into Ray's face, smearing his glasses with her sweat and grease. She started dry humping his leg and he could smell her stale breath. She turned around and started rubbing her thonged ass on his crotch. All Ray actually felt was the material of his pants and his zipper rubbing him raw.

"His cock is getting hard now, I bet. You feel his cock hard for you?" Frankie never shut up. Anastasia said nothing in reply. Ray grunted in pain.

Then she spoke. "You come, you owe me 20 bucks."

"I didn't, no," Ray grunted out.

"Good," she replied. She turned back around and knocked Ray's face again with her breasts.

"Those tits! Smell those big titties!"

"Shut up, Frankie," the girl said.

"I know how to shut you up," he said. "With a cock in your mouth! Yes? You like to suck cock!"

"Christ, Frankie, can I just sell you the damn pictures?" Ray pushed Anastasia away from him.

"My girlfriends not good enough for Ray, huh? Ray's got high class pretty bitches, he doesn't need my dirty whores!"

"Hey, fuck you!" the other girl said.

"Shut up and go snort something. Leave the men to business," Frankie said, flipping her a chubby bird. The girls seemed happy to leave. "Listen, Ray, I only kid you. If I could fuck your girls, I would not be here, either. Hey, they ever want to make some real good money —"

"The pictures, Frankie." Ray took the file out of his briefcase (the same one his mom gave him in high school with high hopes of high finance) and handed it over to Frankie.

"Nice titties," he said, looking at the first one. He flipped through, commenting. "Oh, that white girl loves that big black cock! Yes. Good one. Yes. No, this I cannot use. This girl is Chinese."

"I thought maybe —"

"I said 'niggers.' Not 'chinks.' When nerd convention comes to town, I will say 'chinks.' Klan, I say 'niggers.'"

Ray looked uncomfortably at the black man just six feet away getting a lap dance.

"Oh, him?" Frankie noticed. "He is lost in thoughts of fat white ass. Many of these are good pictures, Ray. I can use this one, this one . . ." Frankie was putting photos on the table. Ray looked around again, embarrassed. "Twelve pictures. That's six hundred dollars."

The amount seemed so high that at first Ray almost agreed. "Wait, you said a hundred a picture."

"See, my Ray, he is smart! You see my joke! Twelve hundred dollars it is! Take off your pants so I can swipe my credit card on your asshole!" Frankie laughed that disgusting laugh, phlegm moving all around his respiratory system. "No, I give you cash. Everyone loves cash."

Ray's eyes went wide as he saw Frankie actually pull out twelve hundred-dollar bills. "Jesus, Frankie!"

"Do not worry, my boy. All this pussy in here, who looks at an old man?" He had a point. "You stay? Get more dances?"

"No thanks," Ray said. "Got to get to work early tomorrow."

"Blacks? You get more hot black pics you tell me! All week these rednecks will be here."

"Yeah, OK," Ray said, already standing up.

"Good bye my boy," Frankie yelled. Ray just waved and walked out. It was just after nine o'clock and Ray felt full of energy and life. He remembered Jenny's apartment was actually just a few blocks away, and thought he'd surprise her.

He turned the corner and walked onto one of the more residential streets of the area. This used to be the place to be, back when Fulton Street was something other than a relic. Those days were long gone. The once-prominent homes had become multiple-family low-income residences, mostly black and Spanish families. But tides were turning again. Because middle class artistic types always seek out the cheapest place to live. And once one white art school grad moves in to one of these poor neighborhoods, it's only a matter of a decade or so before no one can afford it anymore.

Thankfully for everyone around, while Jenny may have started the process, this was a neighborhood it would take a long time to gentrify. Like Ray's area, the housing wasn't only cheap, it was cheap enough that even the most street-retarded cracker knew something was wrong.

A couple of blocks later and Jenny's warehouse was in sight. Jenny and a bunch of other folks had converted an old warehouse into an artistic loft space, complete with a multimedia room, exercise room (rarely used), and various artistic studios. It was, no matter how you looked at it, cool. Ray looked up to Jenny's window and saw a figure move jerkily.

"The fuck you doin' here, dick?" Ray heard. Then he felt fire in the back of his head, soon followed by similar pains on his knees, hands, stomach, and before he could recognize any other sources, he was out.

At some point Ray felt something again, like a dull throbbing ache all over his body. He tasted copper and was pretty sure he felt himself throwing up. He was out again.

Needles? At least one. Out.

There was someone there he knew. He was sure of it. Someone important. Someone—out.

He faded in and out like this and he had no way of knowing how many times. Finally, he at one point found himself pretty much in control of his faculties. He was in a sterile off-white room.

He shared a room with a man who coughed into the air freely, handless stubs unable to wield a tissue in societally proper ways. Ray was terrified. He seemed to have lost the ability to comprehend language, because the bikinied lady on television was making no goddam sense whatsoever. He then remembered that if a bikinied lady on television made no sense, she was probably just a news anchor on a Spanish television station.

"*Telemundo*!" he announced in a deep, booming voice.

"*Señor*?" a nurse said from the door. She was a Latin woman, but was not like the Latin nurses featured in one of the magazines under Ray's futon. "*Señor*? Sir? Are you awake?"

"I think so," Ray said. "Where am I?"

"Mary Mother of God Hospital. You were badly beaten, Mr. Brautigan."

"I can tell. How did I get here?"

The nurse went to check his chart. She made a slight humming sound reading through. "Someone called an ambulance. You were found on the street. The police are waiting outside to talk to you. Are you OK? Can I send them in?"

"The police?" Ray wondered where they were when he needed them. He also wondered what he had on him. "My stuff . . ." he started.

"I believe the police have examined your possessions as evidence. I'll send them in."

She left and was replaced by a couple of uniformed Las Vegas cops.

"Mr. Brautigan, I'm Officer Chan. Did you get a look at your assailant?"

Ray thought about it and realized the answer. "Uh, no, actually. I heard him, but I was down before I saw anyone."

"Mmmhmm. We examined your wallet and briefcase," the cop began. There was not going to be an easy way to explain anything in either one of them. "And they were pretty much empty. Found a P.I. license. You dicking around on a case?"

"Uh, no," Ray said, truthfully. "I was actually going to visit a friend."

"You got a friend in that neighborhood? You sure?"

"Yeah, I'm sure. She's an artist."

"Ah, right. Drugs?"

"What?" Ray said, legitimately confused.

"You two do drugs together?"

"No! I mean, we drink, but that's it."

"Why would your friend live in that neighborhood then? She hooking?"

Ray flashed red. "No. She lives there because it's cheap. Are you fucking investigating my life or the motherfuckers who beat me and robbed me?"

"Robbed you? What'd they take?"

Ray realized that if he mentioned the large amount of money he had been carrying, then he'd probably have to talk about where he got it and why he was carrying it. Frankie had never brought up how legal his enterprises were, but Ray had a good idea that it wasn't the sort of things one should talk with cops about. "Yeah," he said, finally. "They took my money."

"How much?" Chan asked.

"I dunno actually. I wasn't keeping track of what I had. Couple hundred dollars? Maybe a little bit more."

"Flashing that kind of money around there gets you beat to shit."

"I didn't flash anything around. I was going to visit a friend and I heard 'What the fuck are you doing here, dick?'"

"Now, when the perp called you a dick, was he referring to your job or your personality?" Officer Chan was a fucking funny guy. He probably did a frustrated stand up act on open mic nights. But he had a point. Ray hadn't thought about that. It could have been a disgruntled former client. The voice seemed slightly familiar, now that he thought of it.

"I don't know, actually," Ray replied.

"What was in your briefcase?" Chan asked.

'Illegally-shot pornography of private citizens,' Ray thought. "Not much, really. I carry it to look important. Some magazines or something," he said. It wasn't a complete and total lie.

The interrogation went on a while, pointlessly. No one in the room had any illusions that anything would be recovered from the evening, or that any wrong would be punished. It was doubtful, even, that anyone thought that anyone else was being completely honest. Every lie was designed to make everyone else's life easier. They were real humanitarians that way.

34

# CHAPTER FIVE

Ray was released a couple of hours later. His suit was torn and bloodied. His money was indeed gone. His briefcase was empty. The sun was bright overhead. It was eleven o'clock. He had a lot of questions to ask a lot of people, but he also had a job to do. Sweet, pretty, mean Amy Gordon had a no-good boyfriend he was going to catch.

Ray's average looks really served him well when doing work like this. Nobody ever noticed him. Unfortunately, he didn't look so average anymore. He looked like the victim of a fairly serious beating. People notice beat-up motherfuckers. They don't really acknowledge them most of the time, but they do notice them. So that ruled out his first impulse of actually going into the video store where Tom worked. There would actually be some subtlety necessary for this job.

Luckily there was a coffee joint that shared the same parking lot. Ray propped himself up at a table at the window facing the video store. He ordered a coffee that hurt to drink, but that hurt distracted from the rest of his body's hurt, so that wasn't so bad. Ray watched the post-lunch shift start to walk in. Same folks that always worked retail. College kids, high school kids, and the occasional old loser. Ray reached into his pocket for the picture of his target. Red hair, meaty face, the kind of Irish guy whose age you'd never be able to guess, and probably his behavior wouldn't give much of a clue, either.

A blue Ford truck pulled up. And out he stepped, strapping bland Americana. Red faced, empty-brained, and a Dave Matthews bumper sticker on the gas guzzler. Ray realized he was being unfair, but this guy didn't deserve a girl like Amy. He had probably had a bunch of girls he didn't deserve in his life. Probably had two, at least, at the time.

Ray knew that he couldn't sit in the coffee shop for eight hours, so he decided to go home, clean up, and come back closer to the end of Tom's shift. He got his bearings in the hot sun. Tourists avoided him on the street, his bloody suit something sure to ruin their Disneyland commercial fuckathon. Locals just shook their head, assuming he was another dumb tourist that did something even dumber than usual.

Cashless, he walked home. Sweat stung the healing areas of broken skin. Someone had done a serious number on him, this much was sure. Ray had been beaten up plenty of times before. He'd never felt like this, though.

When he got home, he stripped down and went straight for the shower. He paused at the mirror and looked with calm disbelief at the bruises sprouting all over his body. His face was pretty unrecognizable, with one eye almost shut and both lips swollen.

The shower hurt and felt good at the same time, especially every time it switched from ice to fire arbitrarily. The stink of old photo chemicals seemed to increase the sting. Drying was a real chore. Every other square foot of skin was more sensitive than a fat girl at prom.

Ray changed clothes to pants and a T-shirt that didn't smell. He was too sore to do anything else, so he sat on his futon and thought. He thought about how typical it was that when he finally got something he wanted, it was taken away. But he tried not to dwell on that. He had to figure some things out first.

Officer Chan was right, as assholes usually are. The question of why he was called "dick" was pretty vital. Ray went over the options in his head. Obviously, he could have just been mugged. It could have been a disgruntled former client. Maybe it wasn't a coincidence that it happened after Frankie gave him money. Maybe someone from the club saw it. Worse, Frankie might not have wanted to actually lose that money. Ray didn't think Frankie was violent, but he didn't really know the fat bastard too well, either.

Ray suddenly remembered that he was going to visit Jenny when this all went down. He remembered seeing something in the window, and he remembered it looked weird. He picked up his phone. They hadn't taken that, thankfully. Probably because it was a few years out of style. He dialed and it rang. "Hey, it's Jenny. Can't make it to the phone right now, so leave me your name, your number, and a mean joke at the beep. Thanks!"

"Yeah, hey, it's Ray. I was actually around your place last night, but, uh, something happened. Listen, are you OK? I haven't heard from you in a long time. I hope you're OK. Um, I'm OK, but I have a lot of shit to talk about. Nothing, uh, nothing, like, about you or something. Just shit. You know. Um, yeah. So call me." Ray left his number again and hung up.

He leaned back and thought of what Jenny would say about how he looked. A Doctor Doom reference, maybe. Or something more obscure. Sometimes he had to only pretend to get her jokes, and then look them up later at an internet café. He wondered if it was her that he saw in the window. The shadow seemed too big. He didn't like the way it moved. What if something was wrong?

Wait, what if that was why he got beat up? Maybe he saw something he shouldn't have seen? Christ, what could she be into? Maybe she was being robbed or something and an outside man had dealt with Ray? That wouldn't explain the previous months of no calls, though.

It could very well be that Jenny had just gotten sick of Ray. Her other friends were certainly cooler, more fun, and more successful. Maybe she didn't want to sit around making retard jokes and talking about old cartoons and board games. Maybe she had hit it big. She was probably hanging out with rock stars and hot guys, all of them doting on her. Darling of the scene, that could easily be Jenny. And Ray was so far removed from the scene that he'd never even know.

But Jenny wouldn't just leave him without saying anything. Something was up. And while Ray thought about what it could be, he drifted off to a pained sleep.

The next thing he knew, it was dark outside. The daytime's salsa music had been replaced by some kind of Spanish hip hop and the bass vibrated him awake.

"Fuck," he said, looking at the clock. Six thirty. He picked his phone up again and called O. "O, it's me."

"Hey, what's going on? You wanna go out?"

"Yeah, in a bit. I need to ask a favor."

"Ah, shit, man. A job? You need a ride?"

"Yeah, I'm sorry, O. But this job pays REALLY well and I really need the money. I got fucking mugged last night."

"Jesus! Hold on, I'll be right over."

True enough, O's old black Mustang was pulling into the parking lot soon. Ray grabbed his camera and got in the passenger seat.

"Jesus Christ, Ray. You look like fucking hell. A client do this?"

"I don't know, really. I was outside of Jenny's place and somebody jumped me. I don't know who. They either thought I was an asshole or a detective."

"Either way they're right," O laughed.

"Thanks. Thanks. Anyway, they fucking took twelve hundred bucks from me!"

"Shit! Where'd you get that kind of money?"

"Frankie," Ray said, shame evident.

"Did you . . .did you pose for him?"

"What? Fuck! No! Jesus. I sold him some old photos. Turn right. We're going to the Video House on Macabee Street."

"Jesus, Ray. I'm sorry. That really sucks. You tell the cops?"

"They were asking about it, but I didn't want to explain anything about Frankie. I'm embarrassed enough that you know I work with him, let alone, you know, the fucking government. That's a mark on my record I'd rather avoid."

They pulled into the parking lot a bit after seven. "So what's the job? Tailing some porno freak?"

"No. Well, I dunno, maybe he's a porno freak. But this girl hired me to check her boyfriend out. Thinks he's cheating. Though God knows why he would."

"She hot?" O asked.

"Yeah. My first hot client. In the books it happened all the time. I bet your dad had hot clients all the time. Oh, man, she's so pretty."

"Ray's got a crush! Ray's got a crush!"

"God. Are we ever going to grow up?" Ray asked, smiling. "Still, it's hands off."

"Why?"

"She's a client. I don't think that would be a good idea."

"Why, it's not like people hire you more than once."

O had a good point. But something still seemed vaguely treacherous about the whole thing. It felt low, unfaithful. It didn't make sense, but that's how it felt. "There, there he is," he pointed towards the door, glad for the reprieve.

"That meathead? What a dork."

"Yeah, she's totally wasted on him. OK, now remember, be subtle. Nobody ever thinks anyone's going to follow them, so he won't notice unless we're real stupid."

"Can we have a theme song? Wah wah pedals and shit? Or is that too old school?"

"Jesus Christ. Just drive, Kato."

"Bruce Lee was Chinese!" O protested, but drove anyway. It became clear early on that Tom was not going back to the apartment he shared with Amy. He was going to a much nicer neighborhood. It actually made things a little bit harder. Traffic dies down in ritzier spots. Was Tom fucking a rich chick on the side? Did she pay for the new truck?

"Why can't we ever have a real car chase?" O whined. He did a pretty good job following him, Ray realized. They'd done this a few times, and he got better every time. And he didn't even ask for gas money. Tom pulled into a driveway and O just kept going around the block. Once he got to the corner, Ray told him to stop. They watched Tom get out of the truck and go to the house. An older man opened the door and hugged Tom.

"Dead end," O said. "It's his dad."

"Maybe," Ray said. "I'm gonna get out here, I'll be right back." Ray quietly got out of the car and made his way to the house Tom had gone in. The suburbs were certainly ritzier, and the security in the houses was better, but no one ever looked outside. Ray had no problem getting to the house and sneaking around back. Sure enough, the telephoto lens confirmed his suspicions when he looked upstairs. That wasn't Tom's dad, all right. That was Tom's sugar daddy. Ray snapped half a roll of pictures, making sure to get enough clear, explicit shots and then snuck back out of the house's back yard.

He went back to O's car and got in. "Gay," Ray said.

"Hi, Homo," O replied.

Ray laughed even though it hurt. "No, Tom. He's gay. They're lovers."

"You saw them?"

"Yeah. Took pictures."

"You got a fucked up job, man."

"Yeah, I know. Christ, how do I show this to Amy?"

"I dunno, man, but I hope you get some. Sounds like this girl probably needs it," O said, and Ray thought about how bad Amy wanted to get laid. Ray didn't like thinking about that, though.

"Hey, could we drop by Jenny's? I wanna see if she's OK."

"If **she's** OK? Dude, you got mugged last night. She hasn't called you in weeks—"

"Months, actually," Ray corrected painfully.

"I like Jenny, too, man, but I think it's time to leave that behind. If she wanted to hang out, she'd call. Dropping by her house is, it's a little creepy, Ray."

"What, I can't drop by my friend's house to see if she's OK? Just cause she's a girl? I thought I saw something weird in her window last night."

"Conversation over, Ray. You're beat up and fucked up and you need some pussy like crazy. You're not going to Jenny's tonight. You're going home."

Ray recognized the tone in O's voice and knew its inevitability. There was no changing his friend's mind at this point. And maybe he was right. Ray felt like shit, and staying up all night talking with Jenny wasn't going to help that. "Yeah, OK," he said. He touched his bruised ribs and grimaced. "Man, getting beat up fucking sucks."

"Booze in the glove compartment. Don't tell Soph." Ray opened and found a fifth of Maker's Mark.

"Yay," he said and took a swallow. "Shit!" He realized. "I drank from the bottle, I'm sorry."

O smiled. "Oh, well, looks like we gotta finish it tonight. Don't want to waste good bourbon." They drove back to Ray's apartment. It was cramped, but O didn't seem to mind sitting on the floor. "Puts me in touch with my heritage, Brautigan-san."

They passed the bottle and didn't bother with cups. Any germs either one of them had would be killed by the alcohol, anyway. "Remember that time," Ray said, "where we had the Empire, Cobra, and the Decepticons team up with Lex Luthor and Doctor Doom?"

O laughed. "Shit, that was a crazy fucking battle! It all came down to Captain Marvel and Snake Eyes."

"And did the team supreme kick evil ass? Yes, yes they did." Both men laughed and Ray grabbed his side.

"It's funny," Ray said. "When I think of that time, I don't think about worrying if Hollie 'liked me' or something, even though I know I worried about it every day. I think about the good stuff."

"Yeah. I guess that's a human brain thing. We remember the good stuff most."

"What the fuck am I going to remember about this shit when I'm old?" Ray pondered aloud.

"Dude, you'll be lucky to *get* old at this rate."

"Here's to it," Ray said. "Here's to swimmin' with bowlegged women."

"Rather have a bottle in front of me than a frontal lobotomy," O said. They drank up.

Ray winced at the burn of the whiskey on the cuts in his mouth. He felt the clouding of his mind and knew he was going to be talking for a while. "I dunno, O. I'm worried."

Ogami sighed deeply, and not for show. "I know, man. Things haven't been what we thought they'd be, not for a while."

"It's not that. I'm worried about Jenny."

The room was silent. Ogami took another swig from the bottle. "Dude! Enough with her! Shit! Months! She hasn't even fucking called you in months. She was fun as fuck, yeah, I know. And she was hot. But sometimes girls just don't want to be around anymore and they don't know how to say it. Sometimes people are just like that. It sucks but it's true."

"But what . . .what if there's a reason she hasn't called? Like, other than that. This is a shitty city, there's a lot of stuff that happens here. What if something happened to her? I think . . .I think she'd call if she could. She wouldn't do this."

Ray looked around his room.

"Yeah, maybe," Ogami said. "Listen, this weekend, we'll check her out. We'll see what's going on. I just . . .don't get your hopes up, man. Not all friends last a long time."

"Cool," Ray said. "This bourbon's good."

"It's OK," Ogami said. "We'll get the real good stuff this weekend, regardless. You say this Amy girl's paying you good?"

"Yeah, a hundred dollars a day!"

"Shit, that's great! Aw, but you, like, broke the case tonight. That's just, how many days?"

"One," Ray said. "Two if she counts yesterday when she hired me. Well, that's two hundred dollars."

"Maybe you could not tell her for a while. Spread it out, get some more money."

Ray thought about it and he definitely needed the money. "No," he decided. "I think she deserves better than that."

"Good point, maybe if you show her right away you'll get some right away." Ray laughed with Ogami.

"She's probably just a college kid, maybe just graduated. Too young."

"Hm," O said. "Young girls have nice bodies, but they don't know how to fuck yet. And if they do, there's something crazy about them. And crazy can be fun, but I don't think you need crazy, bud."

"I need something," Ray said. "I need something."

# CHAPTER SIX

The next morning, morning being a relative term at this point, Ray wasn't sure if the headache was from the beating some guy gave his body or the beating he gave his own liver the night before. There was a note from Ogami on the door.

> *Hey, Gay,*
> *Had practice today, so I bailed this morning. We're on for this*
> weekend.
> *Stay away from Cobra Commander.*
> *Love,*
>
> *Homogami.*

Ray chuckled and lit an off-brand cigarette. He opened an off-brand Pop tart and ate it without heating it up. He took his phone and called Amy.

"Hello. You've reached Amy Gordon. Please leave your name and number at the beep. Have a nice day!"

"Yeah, this is Ray Brautigan. I'm, uh, calling about the, uh, job we talked about. I've got some, uh, more information for you, uh so, call me back. It's pretty, um, important." Ray still hated fucking answering machines.

Another miserable shower followed by the stench of photo chemicals all throughout his bathroom and Ray started developing the Tom pictures. The funny thing was Tom looked really happy in the photos. So did the older guy. And not just during the sex. They looked happy. Like O and Soph. Ray wondered why Tom felt he had to pretend to be something he isn't. It seemed to Ray that if you found someone you love, you shouldn't act otherwise.

Ray's musings were interrupted by the phone ringing.

"Brautigan," he answered.

"Hey, it's Amy," the phone answered back. "Got your message. God, you're a dork!"

"Uh, what? I hate answering machines. All that pressure to say something concise and clever. If I was good at doing that I'd write for Hallmark."

Did she laugh? She laughed. "Weirdo. Anyway, let's get together for drinks. If you've got something already, I'm going to need a few, I bet. I can meet you at three thirty, same bar. That OK?"

"Um, yeah, I can do that," Ray replied. "Oh, hey, listen, I'm going to look like crap, so don't worry. Just pretend I'm a monster or something."

"Wild night? Maybe we can have one tonight, too."

"Uh, a little too wild. I got beat up," Ray said before thinking, *'Wait, was she coming on to me?'*

"That's awful! Did Tom—?"

"No, nothing to do with Tom. I'm pretty sure. Anyway, I just wanted to warn you. I'm uglier than usual. But, uh, we can, um," Ray stumbled. He really wanted to get back to the previous train of conversation.

"Don't worry, Ray, drinks are on me, tonight. I'll see you at three thirty! Gotta go, bye."

Ray looked at his phone and realized this was as close as he'd come to a date in longer than he'd care to admit. But it wasn't a date. It was very important to remember that. Amy was a client. And she had a boyfriend. He was gay and a liar, yes, but he was her boyfriend. That's why it felt like cheating, probably. It had to be.

Ray went back to his bathroom and hung the better photos to dry. Binder clips on a curtain rod.

He stepped back out and smoked another cigarette, looking down at the squalor in which he lived. There was a framed photo still propped up against a wall. One of his own. He could never bring himself to hang it up, it just seemed so pretentious. He realized that his fridge was covered with photos he and his friends had taken, but little automatic cameras at parties and a shot you could have once sold to a collector for a couple grand seemed to be worlds apart.

Besides, Ray was pretty sure that the walls couldn't really hold up anything. Ray took his phone out again and looked at it. He wanted to call Frankie about as much as he wanted to squeeze the pimples on Frankie's ass, but it was better than actually going to see him. Ray wasn't sure exactly what he should say, though. "Did you have a guy kick my ass and take your money back?" seemed to be a bit direct. And everything else seemed to be a bit retarded.

Ray had taken an improv class while he was in art school. He had seen some sketch comedy on TV and thought it looked fun. What Ray quickly realized is that no one funny takes comedy classes. Fucking shitty losers that think they're funny take improv classes. They do "wild" things and act very "outrageously." You can never tell what "fucking annoying" thing they'll do next, except a good general prediction of "Not be funny."

Ray had tried to avoid improvising anything ever since. But with a pit in his stomach like when he brought home a D in math, Ray dialed without much of a plan.

Someone, maybe Frankie, answered. Ray couldn't understand what was said. "Uh, hello? Frankie? It's Ray Brautigan."

"Huh? Oh! Ray Brautigan! Pussy-lover and chick-fucker! My boy, Ray Brautigan! How are you doing?"

"Um," Ray began, "I—"

"Did you find more hot black fuck pics? Lawn jockeys bending over accountants on golf fields?" Sometimes Frankie was so disgusting he didn't make any goddam sense at all.

"Uh, no, not yet. Listen, Frankie, I got mugged." Ray plunged in.

"Oh, no! That is terrible, my son! You see the fucker who did this?" The concern sounded about as real as anything Frankie ever said did.

"No, I didn't."

"You are OK?"

"Yeah," Ray said. "I guess. I'll live and I'm not missing any organs. But they robbed me blind."

"What all did they get? Did they get your camera?"

"No, no camera, thank shit. They got my money. All of it. Right after I left you." Ray waited and listened.

Frankie paused.

"They took all the money I paid you, this is what you are saying?" Frankie's mood could not be read.

"Uh, yeah."

"The night I gave it to you? Of course. You would not be so stupid as to carry it around for longer. You did not see who did this?"

"No," Ray's stomach quivered and he wanted to shit diarrhea.

"God fucking dammit shit whore fuck ass piss shit fucker faggot fuck bastard fucker fuck fuck!" Frankie screamed some more in another language, and Ray was sure the content was comparable. "Two-bit small time punks! Fucking taking money from my boy! I find this worthless shit, I plant my dick in his eye socket BEFORE I kill his family!"

Ray was suddenly even gladder he never mentioned to the cops what exactly was stolen. He was beginning to regret mentioning it to Frankie. But he was pretty sure, now, that Frankie had nothing to do with it.

"You ever find this asshole shit fucker again, you tell me. You do that for me, Ray Brautigan?"

"Yeah, sure, Frankie, I will, but I hope I never see him again."

"This is to be understood. I am sorry you heard my anger. I do not want one of my best photographers to be fucked by an asshole who knows no shit. I want him only to be fucked by his hot bitches!" And with that, Frankie was back to what passed for normal in Ray's life. "Listen, Ray, my boy. I cannot just give you that money back. It is bad business. I wish I could, but that was a lot of bucks and I have other people to pay, too. But I will try to throw you some extra work, because you deserve a break. Can you do some studio work for me maybe?"

"Uh, what kind?" Ray really wasn't sure where this was going. Well, he knew it would be something filthy, but he wanted to make sure it wasn't anything illegal.

"Ray! You know me! I would do nothing horrible! I always say, 'No animals, no kids.' Not for Frankie! I do not hurt people, I just get them to be hornier!" Ray tried to put the memory of hearing that in the same place he put seeing his parents fuck.

"Um, OK. Yeah."

"I will let you know when I know, OK, my boy Ray?"

"Yeah. Uh, thanks, Frankie."

Ray hung up. Frankie was a nasty piece of shit and he didn't like the idea of having to actually be thankful for him. But, extra cash was always handy. Especially since the Amy job was clearly done. Two hundred wasn't anything to shit on, but more sure would have been nice.

Amy. Ray hadn't shaved since his first meeting with her and normally wouldn't shave again until he got too itchy to stand it. He couldn't actually grow a beard — he was too spotty on the cheeks — but he hated shaving, especially since it usually made him break out. Ray had no illusions about his own attractiveness, but he also didn't want to look like a pimply teenager jerking off to dad's Playboys.

So he scooped the photo chemicals back into the bucket where he kept them and washed out his sink. He needed to look good. Professional. He turned the hot water on and lathered his hands up with cheap soap. He lathered his face up and grabbed his shaving cream. He shook it and pressed the top and a dried up bit spurted out. And nothing else.

"Goddammit," he said to the mirror. He looked at his soapy, bruised face. His eye was a bit better, but not by much. His lips were slightly less swollen. He looked at the disposable razor he hadn't disposed of in months. What good was it really going to do? So he'd have less stubble . . .he'd still look like he sassed Mr. T.

And it wasn't like he was in a respectable job to begin with. This girl paid him money to take pictures of her boyfriend getting fucked by some old guy. An Armani suit couldn't class that up. Ray was scum of the Earth . . . lower, really. He was a parasite feeding off the scum of the earth. He put the razor down, rinsed his face, and went back out of his bathroom and grabbed the cheap jug of bourbon. Might as well get a head start.

As he was walking to Cheers, he almost thought about calling O for a ride. He was still sore and truthfully didn't feel up to it. But if O drove him, he'd want to come into the bar and have some drinks. Amy deserved her privacy as much as anyone else. Rather, she deserved to think she had privacy as much as anyone else.

So he trudged his way there and vaguely hoped no one paid much attention to the flask that helped him get there. But this was Vegas, after all, and not even the part where tour-ons fuck everything up. It was the part where Nobody Gives a Shit Period.

# CHAPTER SEVEN

He got there in about half a flask's worth of walking. Not bad. He entered Cheers and almost didn't recognize her. She was wearing plastic monster fangs and pointy ears like Spock or an Elf, depending on what variety of nerd you are. She waved him over and gave the best smile someone with plastic fangs could give.

"Uh, hi," Ray said, confused. "What's, uh, what are you . . ."

"You said you'd look like a monster, and I wanted to fit in," she replied. She lifted her scotch and tried to drink. "It's real hard drinking with these things. Let's go to our booth. Send us over another Scotch," she said to the bartender. Not yet recovered, Ray followed dutifully.

By the time they sat down, he was composed enough to say, "You can take those out, Amy. Thanks for the gesture, even though it's, uh, really weird."

Amy took out her fangs and smiled. "How often does a girl get to dress like a monster? And you don't look that bad. I don't see anything missing. Anything missing I can't see?"

"No. Well, my appendix."

"No appendix? Oh, this just isn't going to work, then."

The bartender came over with another Scotch. Amy paid and tipped fairly well. "What happened, Ray?"

"Oh, uh, I got mugged. I was walking to my friend's apartment and someone jumped me and took all my money and beat, well, you can see they beat the crap out of me."

"Shit," she said, and touched his face. The blushing actually made the pain throb worse. "Wow, you must be really sore. Sorry if I hurt you."

"Uh, no, it's OK. Sorry, uh, sorry I didn't shave," Ray blurted, wondering why he blurted it.

"No, it's good," she replied. "Now you're all 'rugged badass.'"

"A badass wouldn't get his ass kicked."

"You should see the other guy." They both laughed softly and took a drink. "So, uh. See any good movies lately?" she asked after a short pause.

"Not really," Ray replied. He hadn't been able to afford movies in a long time. He recognized what Amy was doing. A lot of clients did it. They used small talk to put off seeing what their significant other was up to. It was usually boring and pathetic. This time it felt kind of nice, but Ray knew it was for the wrong reasons.

He glanced at her hand and noticed her fingernails. He always did. No nail polish, but well-groomed. Nail polish, ever since he was a child, made him uncomfortable. Blood red fingers on his mom's hands for special occasions, there was something wrong about it to him.

At this point the silence was as painful as his headache. "So, uh, your case," he said.

Amy sighed and looked away. "Yeah. I shouldn't waste your time. It's just . . .I dunno if I'm ready. It's bad news, isn't it?" She looked at him and her eyes were wide and clear. Ray nodded his head.

"Fuck," she said simply. She downed the rest of her Scotch in one gulp and signaled for another. Ray knew to wait. He couldn't imagine how much he was about to hurt this poor, beautiful girl. He felt layers of guilt smothering him, like blankets from an overprotective aunt.

She got her other Scotch and downed it in two gulps. Another signal, another drink. When the bartender left this time she said, "OK. Let's see what you have."

Ray handed a manila folder over carefully. He looked away as she opened it. She took out the pictures. She looked at them, one by one, carefully. Ray couldn't figure out where to look.

"He's gay," she said finally. "Tom's gay." Ray wasn't sure if she was looking for a response.

"Yeah," he tried. He waited. Tears? Anger? His nervousness threatened to physically manifest.

"Oh, thank God." She smiled a bit.

"Uh, what?"

"Oh. Yeah, that might seem weird. Listen, I've been busting my ass trying to turn this guy on. Lingerie, fantasy stuff, porno, asking for other girls to come home with us, I've tried everything. And Tom, well, he didn't show much interest in anything. Typical girl, I couldn't bare to blame anyone but myself. I thought there was something wrong with me. Tom didn't want to fuck me because I still wasn't sexy enough, or fun enough, or something. All the while I knew I was being stupid, but I couldn't help it. That ever happen to you?"

"Yeah," Ray knew without thinking. He called that "life."

"So, you know, this is a relief, in a way. I mean, I'm pissed at this lying piece of shit coward, but at least this means that guy that wouldn't fuck me no matter what I did, well, he was gay. He's gay!

There's nothing wrong with me! Oh, God. Yay," she said, but not all that enthusiastically.

And the hard part never gets easier. "So, uh—" Ray began.

"What are your plans for tonight?" Amy asked.

"Um. Nothing. Yeah, uh, nothing, really."

"Great. Stay here with me and drink. It's on me."

"I don't think that's, uh, that's really very appropriate."

"Why?"

"Well, you're my client," Ray said.

"You're fired."

Ray paused for a moment. He didn't have much leg to stand on from here. "I, uh, I don't think—"

"Are you gay?" Amy asked tersely.

"No!"

"Then I suggest that you do **not reject me** right now and you sit here and get drunk with me. Come on, I can tell you like drinking. And you're funny. And I'm funny. We can drink and be funny together. Please."

She looked at him with a smile, but he seemed to see that she really meant it.

"Yeah, OK," Ray said, already feeling guilty. The guilt flashed away in a hot wave as she grabbed his hand.

"Yay! Thanks, Ray. You're sweet."

They drank. They drank and they talked and Ray lost himself in it. That feeling of new friendship, the same as a new love affair, it's that excitement to get everything out onto the table. Movies you love. The seminal stories of your life. Why you have that scar. First loves, first heartbreaks. That crazy guy you knew in high school. There's a joy in sharing these things for the first time with a new person that's hard to match. In the back of his head, Ray, having not felt it in such a long time, wondered if this is why people cheated: not for the sex, but for this.

He told her about the time he and O got locked inside the mall when they were 16. She told him about how she preferred action figures to dolls as a girl. They talked about music, sharing loves, chiding disagreements, and, enough drinks into the night, singing along to the jukebox. It was at this point that Ray realized that he couldn't be at Cheers anymore. There were no songs worth singing there. There had to be singing. He looked around and he was at the Hole in the Wall Bar again.

Immediately, an anxiety attack began. He'd brought a client to his actual bar. This was bad. He never did this.

But, "THE FINAL COUNTDOWN!" Amy sang along. And he forgot about his worries and joined in for the "Doo do doo doo's."

There was a sudden inexplicable anger when he saw Chief Black Ass chatting Amy up. He grabbed her by the shoulders and returned her to the juke box with him, saying something about needing help deciding.

Ray later noticed they were back alone at a booth. They were on the same side. They were talking very closely. He could smell her shampoo and it was apple-y. He wasn't sure what she was saying sometimes, or if she was saying anything, but they were both laughing.

At some point they must have left. They were walking in the cool night air of Las Vegas. Ray saw a ketchup bottle he'd just thrown on the ground. Amy was doubled over in laughter.

"Thanks, Ray," Amy said.

"No problem that ketchup sucked!" Ray kind of thought he said.

"No, really. Thanks for tonight. I had a lot of fun. Chief Black Ass is a riot!"

"Yeah, he's OK," Ray sat down, the joy of the night drained immediately.

Amy rested her head on Ray's shoulder and he felt himself break out into a cold sweat.

"You're the best dick I know," Amy giggled. "If I pay you now, will you feel like a hooker?"

Ray suddenly felt very, very sober. His mind raced, trying to figure out the implications of this statement. *'Was it flirting was it a joke was she coming on to me are we going to fuck oh God this isn't right we're cheating I'm cheating but I don't and she doesn't oh God that apple smell she's soft her T-shirt her breasts those silly Spock ears oh God.'* "Uh, no, it's OK." After all that thought, that's all that came out.

Amy got up and handed Ray a wad of cash. "That's with tip, since I dragged you out all night."

"Thanks," Ray felt unable to talk about what was going on. "Um."

"We could have a nightcap at my place, since Tom's probably not coming home. But I have to go to school tomorrow morning."

College girl, Ray knew it. Ray wasn't ready to leave, wasn't ready for Amy to leave. But he also wanted her to leave. He felt uncomfortable. Something was wrong. But he also wanted her. He stood up next to her and she hugged him and kissed him on the cheek. The corners of their lips touched and Ray's dick twitched.

Ray's mind and blood raced. He returned the embrace and worried about holding it for too long. He was getting hard and felt ashamed. *'College girl. Too young. Cheating on Jenny.'* Ray knew he couldn't cheat on Jenny. But he had to say something. *'College girl. Shit.'*

"So, uh, what's your major?" Ray cursed himself like a livid fiend. The most boring question anyone in college ever hears. He hated himself with fierce passion.

"Huh? Oh, no, no major. I'm not in college yet. I'm still in high school, doofus!"

Ray said nothing as his mind was flooded with thoughts and feelings. His dick remained slightly stiff.

Amy started to walk off. "Hey, can I give you a call sometime? I really did have fun tonight."

Ray nodded dumbly and still couldn't help but watch her body walk away in the night light. He immediately began berating himself. *'Jesus fuck! A fucking kid! A fucking high schooler! I want to fuck a teenage girl! What's wrong with me? Am I a pedophile? Jesus. What's wrong with me? Oh, man. But, the way she feels, and that body, and when it's against me and that kiss, that felt good . . .but she's a teenager! She could be half my age! She might be less! Oh, God.'* As Ray walked home the interior monologue continued on more or less the same path.

He sat at a bus stop and the next thing he knew he was on his futon, too drunk to jack off.

# CHAPTER EIGHT

Morning came. And went. Ray's bladder awoke him sometime around noon. After a long, painful morning piss he retreated to his futon and sat down, slumped over. He did everything he could to think of something other than the previous night. He actually cleaned his apartment. He looked at the Spanish calendar he had found on the street and remembered that Ogami's band had a show that night. Ray knew he could use the distraction.

He walked over to his pants and took his phone out to charge it. That was something he could never remember to do while drunk. As he took the phone out he saw that he had a message. Despite himself, he excitedly opened the phone and called his voicemail. Not many people had his number, but Jenny did.

"Hey, my boy," Frankie's voice was even less welcome than usual. "I told you I would get you some good work and I have done that for you. You give me a call back today and you'll be earning some real money, eh! That's what Frankie does for his Ray boy!"

Ray tried to think hopefully about the situation. He tried to pretend that maybe this would be some really hot girls doing something really sexy. Not classy, but maybe Frankie had really struck the jackpot this time. Also, maybe they shat gold and had diamond boogers.

His stomach could take no more delay. He pulled on his pants and one of his less dirty t-shirts and walked out, knowing his body would feel disgusting as soon as it hit the sunlight. Hunger trumped hygiene once again for Ray Brautigan.

Across the street was a Mexican deli with a possibly legal kitchen. The old *abuelitas* behind the counter stared at Ray, as they always did. "Uh, *hola*," he managed. Three years of high school Spanish and all he remembered was "fart" and "dick." "Um, Yo kee-air-oh dos tacos con, uh, cho-ree-zo. Please."

The grandmas nodded and chattered to each other while they got to work. Ray picked out a Mexican Coke. Sweeter, just exactly what no one really needs for breakfast. A couple of *cholos* gave Ray a double take as they entered the deli. Ray sniffed his pits and realized that, for once, it wasn't because he was white. Soon enough the Mexican sausage would overpower any personal odor.

One of the grandmas brought the two tacos over. Ray tried picking one up but it burned his fingers and he muttered "Fuck." The grandmas and the *cholos* shared a laugh, so Ray joined them.

*'What's the legal age in Vegas, anyway?'* he found himself thinking. *'Jesus, what's wrong with me?'* Ray knew that few men would judge him for being attracted to a hot teenager. It was, after all, the American way. But it was a phenomenon he'd hated for a long time, probably all the way back to when the high school guys dated all his cute classmates in junior high.

He thought about what Jenny would think. The hell she'd give him just for hanging out with this girl would put Dante to shame. Ray had to admit, the two women . . .girls . . .whatever, they were a bit alike. He wondered what Amy would be like once she got to his age. Would she be Jenny? God, would he even tell Jenny? It might be one to keep under wraps, like the time he called that hooker.

Then Ray remembered that he probably wasn't going to be telling Jenny anything for a while. Or ever. He shook his head and started on his tacos. He and Ogami would drive by her place, find her, and they'd all go out for a wild Saturday. She'd have some great stories to tell.

Or she'd never speak to him again.

The taco was greasy and good. His stomach rumbled a meager protest but he paid it no mind. The Coke did little to alleviate the burns on his tongue from the spicy sausage. He didn't care much. Years of alcohol had rendered his taste buds almost completely inoperative.

A belch yielded an unbelievable combination of unpleasant tastes. He paid his customary five dollars and walked back to his apartment. The stink was beginning to burn his nose. And, of course, he had nothing else to do.

As he lathered his body he remembered the smell of Amy's breath. That moment when the corners of their mouths touched. He started to get hard and thought about masturbating but got mad at himself for being so stupid. He wasn't a sicko and it wasn't time to start acting like one. He knew he should just finish showering and call the black-market porno guy about shooting something possibly illegal for him. Ray did not find the irony amusing in the least.

After he finished drying off, he took the customary "about to call Frankie" shots of bourbon. He wondered if anyone dealt with him sober. As he was downing the second, his phone rang, startling him. Wishing he had caller ID, he hesitated. There were basically only two people he'd want to hear from. Ogami would leave a message. Jenny . . .probably wasn't going to call.

The phone rang again.

If it was Jenny, then she deserved to get his machine. It rang. If it was Jenny, she deserved for him not to answer. She hadn't answered.

But maybe she hadn't answered for a good reason.

It rang again.

It was probably just Frankie. And he needed to call Frankie anyway. And maybe it was . . .

Ray answered, nerves on fire. "Hello?"

"Ray? It's me!"

The reception wasn't good but the voice was female. "Huh?"

"It's me, dorkus!"

Ray's heartbeat got even faster. "Jenny?"

"What? Reception's bad! Ray, are you there?"

"JENNY?" Ray said, louder than he'd planned. "JENNY?" Still too loud.

"Ray, hello? Can you hear me? It's—" and the reception cut out even worse. Ray was covered with sweat. Was this? This was . . .it . . . ." —hear me? Stupid phone! Hold on, I'll call you back in a second."

"No, stay on! Jenny!" but the line was dead.

Ray stared at the phone and he was out of breath. He felt like his mind should be racing, like it did the night before. But it was serene. It was calm. There was nothing. There was awful, painful silence. He could hear his own heart. It was like standing next to Phil Rudd at an AC/DC concert. BOM cha BOM cha BOM cha BOM cha BOM cha.

And the whole time you're thinking, "Come on Angus. Fucking wail."

Finally, the phone rang.

"Hello," he answered without hesitation.

"Ah, finally. Sorry, I was getting bad reception back there. What's up?"

Ray wasn't sure where to begin. So much to catch up on. Should he go with most recent first or . . .wait. That wasn't—who was it?

"Jenny?" Ray tried.

"No, dorkus! It's me, Amy! Hello, the girl with the gay boyfriend you were out with last night!"

"Oh. Ah. Uh, sorry."

"Who's Jenny? Is she your giiiiiirlfriend?" Amy teased.

"No! She's a good friend of mine."

"Ray has a girlfriend, Ray has a girlfriend! Oooooo!"

Ray was surprised that he laughed. It was actually really annoying him, but he couldn't help it. "I don't have a girlfriend. Shut up."

"Well, good. I can steal you again tonight. It's Friday and I want to actually go out for once and not worry about Gay Tom."

"Uh, I actually, uh, I have plans, Amy." This was, for once, true.

"Yeah, what are you doing? Got a big case? A murder?"

"No, no, nothing like that," Ray replied. Ray investigating a murder would be like a high school baseball umpire heading a senate investigation on fundraising corruption or whatever those things investigated. "My friend's band is playing tonight at Stinky's."

"Stinky's? Where's that?"

"Um, uh, downtown." Ray wasn't sure if this was small talk or an interrogation.

"So I can come along, right? I like music. What kind of music?"

"Uh, it's just rock and roll, I guess. But, um, I don't think it's that great of an idea for you to, uh, come with me."

"Why?" Amy's question left little room to dodge.

"You're, uh, you're in high school, Amy." Why wasn't this obvious to her? Why did it fall to him to say this? It was embarrassing.

"Well, not tonight. And tomorrow's Saturday. So what's your point?"

"It's, uh . . ." the words were slippery like soap in prison. " . . .uh, inappropriate."

"I'm not your client anymore. No business problems there. We're old pals now." Amy wasn't whining, she was merely putting her case forward. Amy probably often got her way.

"It's . . .it's illegal, Amy! Jesus, you're, what, 16?" Ray couldn't take it anymore.

"First off, it would only be illegal if we fucked. Are we going to fuck, Ray?"

Ray turned bright red even though she wasn't around.

"You just turned bright red, didn't you?"

" . . .No," Ray really had nothing else he could say.

"Yes, you did. I heard you turn bright red. It sounded like sssswwwooooooooooob. Anyway, it would only be illegal if we fucked, and since you didn't say we were going to, I guess we're not. Second, it would not be illegal for us to fuck if I were sixteen, it would be illegal for us to fuck if I was fifteen. I'm not sixteen, I'm seventeen, and that means it would, in fact, be legal for us to fuck, and that it would have been legal for us to fuck last year, as well, but we're not going to, so that's a moot point. So I guess we just have that, huh?"

Ray had tried out for debate club once in high school. He was the only guy that got rejected. Rejected from debate club and he never quite understood why until this moment. He found it impossible to refute her. He felt the familiar old feeling of resignation and shrugged his shoulders.

"I don't have a car or anything so I can't pick you up," it was a feeble last attempt and he knew it.

"That's no problem. Who wants to drive, anyway? Can't drink much, then."

At this point, Ray knew better than to bring up the legality of her drinking. Girls like this always had a way and no one dared question them. They were like a high caliber bullet fired from a high powered sniper: when they had an aim, they were going to get there and anything in-between was going to get a nasty hole through them.

"Stinky's you said, right? Gimme the address."

Ray complied without protest.

"OK, Ray. I'll meet you there. When do they go on?"

"Eleven," Ray said. "But, uh, I want to get there early."

"No doubt, gotta get a head start. Meet there at ten? Whoever gets there first gets two seats at the bar." It wasn't a request.

"OK," Ray said.

"Oh, hey, what kind of rock? Is it all glam and shit or what? I gotta know how to dress."

"Uh, it's, rock? Loud and big, the way it's supposed to be. It's not, like, Goth or post rock or anything that has a uniform. Just whatever. I mean, what you wear. It'll look, uh, good, whatever."

"Cool. OK, I'll see you then. Remember, Ray, no fucking. You said so, not me."

Ray stammered a few non words, "Buh, uh . . .um,"

"Did you hear that? Swooooooooob, again. Even brighter red. You gotta work on that if you're gonna roll with me. Bye!"

# CHAPTER NINE

Ray was accustomed to utter defeat by this point, but this was annihilation on a new scale. This wasn't Custer's last stand, it was Custer's last stand against a million killer robot zombies. Still, it was almost comforting.

But that particular phone call had somehow completely countered the effects of the cheap bourbon. He took out a larger glass. Well, glass wasn't really the right word. "Mostly cleaned old Slush Puppy container from a gas station," was a closer fit, but who's counting?

He briefly thought about filling it up and remembered the last time he'd tried that. He and Jenny had slammed down the sugar-filled poison and decided to try to drink just as much liquor. He had bourbon, she had tequila. They didn't even get close to half done before Vomitathon 2002 commenced. The winner of the gold medal was still in hot dispute. Ray laughed as he filled about a quarter of the giant dinosaur-shaped monstrosity with cheap hooch.

He turned the radio on to fill his head. Most of the stations blared the same salsa that his neighbors blared. He found a public station and listened to the news. Same as always. Somebody won something, somebody lost something, and poor people killed each other. Except instead of a lottery, someone won a spelling bee. Instead of losing their celebrity wife, someone lost a battle to keep their book in print. And the poor people didn't kill each other because they were criminals, it was because they were poor and mistreated.

Ray turned the radio off and drank in silence. He wondered what exactly he'd gotten himself into, but had to admit it was better that sitting on his futon alone drinking. After a half hour or so, calling Frankie seemed bearable. So he did.

"Hello, this is Frankie." He picked up fast.

"Yeah, uh, Frankie. It's Ray. Ray Brautigan."

"Ray my boy! You are ready for some money, yes? And no fucking Mex boy is going to steal it from you this time, I guarantee it! Good money, and you can have some fun while making it! This is a good life we lead, Ray Brautigan my boy."

"Uh, right. So, uh, what do you need?" Frankie's monologues rarely gave way to an appropriate response.

"You come meet me at Melanie's," Ray's heart sank a bit further. "Do not worry, though, we will not stay there. We go to location from there, you take some good photos for me, you get some money, you look at some nice views, and you buy your fuckfriends nice presents and condoms."

Again, what does one say to that? "Uh, what time?" was the best Ray could do.

"You come over at five o'clock tonight. We are like Batman and Dracula, we work at night best. You are Batman and I am Dracula! Ha ha, it is because of my accent and you are detective!"

There was a specific amount you should drink to prepare for talking to Frankie. Too little and you're aware of how much you hate yourself and your life and Frankie. Too much and it confuses the shit out of you when he starts going on and on. "Uh, right."

"I will see you then, my boy! Say, what kind of girl you like?"

"What?"

"What kind of girl you like? You like hot teenage action?"

"NO!"

"Whoa now Ray Brautigan, my boy, do not yell. Some guys like the teen fuck pictures, barely legal. Other guys, they like the big giant titties to suck on. Some guys, they like Spanish girls with big butts and some guys like Asian girls with their sideways pussies!"

"What?" Ray really regretted asking, but it just came out.

"It is joke. Chinese girls have normal pussies, do not worry. Just asking to see what you like, maybe I can get some for our photography night session."

"Uh . . .I dunno. What do you mean 'get?'" Ray worried aloud.

"I pay many girls different times! I am just wondering if you want to work with a specific type and I will help you out! What do you like? Titties? Asses? You like the anal whores?"

Ray liked pretty girls that joked around with him. "I dunno, whatever," he answered.

"You like them all, yes, Ray Brautigan? You fuck all hot pussies because you are Ray Brautigan my boy!"

This seemed to be the answer that would satisfy Frankie. "Uh, yeah," Ray managed.

"Ha ha ha ha! If I were your age I would fuck all the girls, too! See you at ten! Be careful, do not fuck my girls so hard they do not want pictures anymore, just the picture man! Ha ha ha ha ha ha! Good bye my boy!"

Ray sometimes wondered if Frankie was just very clueless, very friendly, or a deeply sarcastic asshole. He dialed Ogami's number. It rang a few times.

"Hey, yo," O answered.

"O, it's Ray."

"No shit. You have your own ring on my phone. Want to know what it is? It's the A-Team theme."

"I love it when a plan comes together."

"You coming to the show tonight, Ray? Gonna be a good one."

"Yeah. Hey, who's opening?"

"It was going to be Sgt. Rawk but now it's Action Friend Force."

"Aw, man. I hate those guys. Totally just ripping off Tenacious D."

"They're OK. They're just a couple of nerds. But you don't have to get here for them. We go on at eleven, probably a bit late. Stinky's is never organized. Imagine that, a place called 'Stinky's' not being very organized."

"Yeah, shocking. No, I'll get there at ten. I gotta meet someone."

There was a pause. "Really?"

Ray realized he was embarrassed about a second too late. "Uh, yeah. Just this client. Uh, former client."

"Wait, that Amy girl? With the gay boyfriend? You fucked her, didn't you? What'd I tell you?"

"No, I didn't fuck her! We just hung out and we're going to, uh, again tonight."

"So you're going to fuck her tonight? I'll give off the sex vibe if you want. Everybody gets laid when I do my Wave Cutting Sex Stance."

"No, I'm not going to fuck her! She's seventeen! A fucking kid!"

"You are a filthy pervert and you disgust me," O replied.

"Shut up," Ray wittily replied. "She made me agree to meet her. Who else is coming? Please don't tell anyone she's that young. I feel like shit already."

"Soph will be there. Adam, John, I dunno, those kind of folks."

Ogami had a lot more friends than Ray did. "Should I call — oh," Ray interrupted himself.

Ogami audibly sighed on the other line. "Listen, I'll call her and see if I can get through. Remember, we're going there tomorrow afternoon. Then we either all have a good time or you drop it."

"Right," Ray said. He was still getting used to the idea. He didn't have many friends, and never really had. He was an only child, too. Friendship, to Ray, was an even more sacred bond than family. It was chosen, and once it was chosen, you don't turn your back on it, no matter what. It hurt to think someone had turned her back on him, but it hurt even worse to do it right back. "Anyway, I'll see you there. And I swear to shit, you better not say anything about this kid."

"Is she hot?"

"What?" Ray heard perfectly well, but he didn't like the question.

"You heard me. Is she hot?"

"I dunno, she's a kid."

"I didn't ask if you were going to marry her and live with her and her folks. I asked if she's hot. Some girls are, some aren't. Is she?"

Ray thought about it. He didn't really have to think hard, but he didn't want to admit it. "Yeah. She is."

"SICKO! PERVERT! PEDOFREAK!"

"ARRRGH!" Ray shouted, in only half mock-irritation. "SHUT UP!"

"Heheheh, see you tonight, bud. Stay gay."

"You too."

Ray went to the mirror and wondered how professional one needed to look for an underground pornography photo shoot. Then he remembered his only suit was torn to shit and that looking professional wasn't an option anymore. His face was healing, but he still looked like hell.

So, old cargo pants and a T-shirt it was. He pulled on the ratty sneakers that needed replacing more desperately than a colostomy bag and headed out to Melanie's.

# CHAPTER TEN

The bus was late and he sat on the bench alone for twenty minutes. Public transportation in Las Vegas has a reliability directly proportional to the closeness to the tourist areas. Ray and the other poor folk being shuffled far away from spending eyes, that meant his bus came when it felt like coming. Sometimes that was on time. Others . . .well, it helped to have a magazine.

Ray had no magazine. He had a head full of thoughts that he mostly wished would just get the fuck out. He wondered just how well this job would pay. Frankie seemed to think it was comparable to the twelve hundred that Ray lost. If so, Ray didn't care how fat the "models" were. Money like that could buy him a better ad, a bed, and a lot of other things. And maybe he wouldn't need an ad. Maybe this job would lead to more like it. It wasn't exactly why he went to art school, but it seemed to be less likely to get him beat up than snooping on cheating spouses.

When the bus had arrived, Ray was almost excited about the opportunity. Some part of him reminded the other parts exactly what he was getting excited about, and so that soon passed. Ray didn't think of himself as cynical, really. It wasn't the world that was hopeless or irredeemable. It was his life. He was too close to Ogami to think that no one was happy. Plenty of people were happy. Plenty of people hadn't let their own bad decisions and bad luck drive them into a giant pit of shit. Ray could vaguely remember when he was one of them.

The bus was crowded and smelled like aromatic groceries. He thought about squeezing in next to the fat lady and the old man, but his feet weren't tired enough for the likely stench that seat would provide, so he just held the rail and stood.

Most folks got off at one strip mall or another. Las Vegas' image is that of a glitzy highlife, all crazy architecture and flashing lights. Well, that's a few blocks of the entire city. The rest of the place is approximately 99% strip malls. Tobacco stores, bars, general stores, more bars, more tobacco stores, "massage parlors," pretty much like the entire rest of the country except more filthy.

One by one the more normal passengers filed out at the various strip malls, in search of whatever commerce they thought they needed. Ray realized with a sinking feeling that as time went on, only the weirdest and most desperate looking men stayed on the bus. This was the problem with public transportation: being forced to see who else is going where you're going. Ray looked at the old toothless man, the fat guy in the stained T-shirt, the shifty, greasy young man who probably wasn't legal, and the obvious crackhead rambling about better times. These, unfortunately, were his people.

By the time his stop had come, Ray was so thoroughly depressed that he almost forgot his camera case. The camera case that held equipment more expensive than the rest of Ray's possessions combined, including, by most accounts, his own life. Thankfully, it was at his feet and instead of outright forgetting it, he nearly stumbled over it, causing the crackhead untold amounts of hilarity. Ray almost flipped the bird, but remembered how scared he was of crackheads. Motherfuckers didn't give a shit about anything.

As he walked up to Melanie's, Ray only got more depressed when the bouncer recognized him. Ray, at one time, had always enjoyed being a regular somewhere. The bartenders treated you better, you always had friends there, and you knew the best thing to order at any time. At no time did Ray ever want to be a regular at a two-bit strip joint. Ray didn't ever want to be a regular at any sort of strip joint. It wasn't that naked women bothered him, or even unattractive naked women. Like on the bus, Ray didn't like to be reminded who he was. At a strip club, Ray would invariably look around and notice the various losers and freaks collected within. Blessed with less self-awareness, they sat and enjoyed their show, while Ray could only think, *'Oh, God. Is that me? These women must hate us all.'*

It never occurred to Ray that the very fact that he obviously thought they hated him certainly helped them do so. When you're ready to be hated, you will be.

Ray wasted no time making his way to Frankie in his usual corner. He was there with Anastasia again and Ray wondered if he should say "Hello." After a look that said, "Who the fuck are you, oh, wait, I don't care," Ray decided against a greeting.

Frankie, of course, did not. "Ray Brautigan my boy! Here you are, ready for work! Ha ha! Frankie is your big boss now, eh? I want expense report by tomorrow! I kid, I kid."

Of course he did. Ray doubted that Frankie knew what an expense report was. "You ready?" Ray asked.

"Again, that is my boy, the cold business man. No pussy or tits until business is over for my boy! Ho-kay, let us be on our way. Frankie will drive."

Anastasia interrupted, "Hey, Frankie. We're running out. You got any more?"

Frankie didn't bother looking at her. "You run out because you snort too much. Do you want to ruin that nice Slavic brain? You fucking slow down! I will tell you when you need more, this is understood?"

"Goddammit, you toad, I know you got some!" She had quite a temper.

"Yes, I know I got some, too. I know I gave you plenty for two or three weeks and you snort it in three nights. I know you get jack of shit from me for those two or three weeks. You learn to snort right or you don't snort at all, end of conversation." The jovialness gone from Frankie's voice, when he said, "end of conversation," it really was. Frankie got up and waddled towards the exit and Ray followed, avoiding eye contact with, well, everyone. Frankie led the way to an old Buick *Lesabre*.

As they climbed in, Frankie was happy again. "You like my classic American car? Some say 'old' but I like 'classic' better. Sure, it is no fifty-seven Chevy with nice fins, but this car is big and the engine is big and it is ready to take us to Fucktown!"

Ray's immediate impulse was to open the door and jump out of Frankie's already-moving car. The facts suddenly sobered him: he had just climbed into a car with a creepy little underground porn magnate going to a place only said creepy little underground porn magnate knew of. On top of this, no one else knew he was doing this. Ray suddenly had the terrifying thought that this was going to be the beginning of a very bad horror movie. "So, uh, where we going?"

"Oh, my boy Ray, not far. My house is too far away for this one, so I have arranged another location."

Ray wasn't sure which was worse: Frankie's house, or "another location."

"Uh, where?" he prodded. '*Nice detective work, jackass,*' he added inwardly.

"Oh, it is close. You will flip your shit when you see what we have!"

It turned out Frankie was right, but perhaps for reasons he would not have predicted. They pulled into the parking lot of a video store. The video store where Amy's gay boyfriend Tom worked. "Here?!" Ray asked, shocked.

"Yes! I give manager a little gift, he closes shitty store early on Friday for 'repairs.' Next thing you know, hot pussies and cocks fucking all over video store and you are the big photo man for all of it!"

"That's so fucking weird," Ray said. "I was just here the other day."

"Oh? You rent movie here?"

"Huh? No, no VCR. I was, well, it was work. Can't talk about it."

"Of course not. But if you got good hot black fuck pics, you tell me, right? Ha ha ha, I only kid."

"Yeah, OK. Weird. This is just weird." They got out of the car and entered the store. Sure enough, there was Tom, along with another worker and long, thin man who appeared to be the manager. Ray was staring at Tom, but had trouble stopping. He was trying to read his face. Did Amy tell him yet? Did they break up? Ray suddenly felt very angry.

"OK, fellas, it's closing time."

"What?" the other worker asked. It's not even six yet!"

"Don't worry, Doug. You'll get your full pay. These men are here for some, uh, exterminating. Those roaches you were complaining about, Tom?"

Ray was still staring when Tom spoke up. "Oh. Yeah, they were nasty. So we still get paid? You could have told us, Bret."

"What can I say, I like surprises. Go home and fuck that hot girlfriend of yours, what do you care?"

Tom's face flashed almost as red as Ray's. He finally looked over and caught Ray in his stare.

"What's your problem, faggot?" Tom asked.

That was too much. Ray tried to contain a laugh but failed miserably.

"What's his problem?" Tom was getting agitated. "Fucking bug killer, who gives a shit, creepy little fuck!"

"Listen to your boss and get the fuck out of here, Red," Frankie said, stone calm. "I killed bigger bugs than you back home."

You could see a battle on Tom's face, dignity versus fear. Dignity has a glass jaw, though, and Tom gathered his things and left. "Better things to do," he mumbled. The other worker left with him. Bret, the manager, stayed behind.

"OK, Frankie, you break anything here, you pay for it. Twice."

"Of course."

"Leave the keys in my office, I've got a spare set."

"Of course."

"And don't leave no weird stinks on nothing. And I get a free copy of all of it!"

"Of course."

Bret stood still for a bit. "You sure I can't stay and —"

Frankie interrupted. "Bret, friend, you are a good and smart man. But we are professionals. You throw in a nonprofessional, he starts looking at the girls, he starts getting boner, and he goes fuck crazy. Me and Ray Brautigan, we seen enough pussy that we don't give a shit any more. It's a job like any other, and it's hard. You stand and you look at pussy and cock. You do this for hours. It is not dream world where hot bitches suck on your cock while you make pictures of them. You stay here, you go crazy and you go bored, all at same time. So you leave now." Ray was impressed with Frankie's restraint and professionalism. Maybe he wasn't so bad after all.

He was still ugly.

Bret finally nodded and gathered his things. "OK. Remember, keep the blinds shut. Don't want no creepy perverts at the coffee shop getting their rocks off for free and calling public health on me."

"We will be blind bats in here, Bret. Have a good night."

Bret left.

Ray was trying to figure out how best to compliment Frankie.

"Stupid ass!" Frankie said. "Stupid skinny cock! He thinks he gets to watch hot fuck action? He is not real man like Ray and Frankie. We get our cocks sucked and take pictures of it all night!"

Ray sighed. "Frankie, I told you I only could do this until ten or so."

Frankie nodded. "That will be enough. Then I take all the pussies home for myself ha ha ha!"

"Yeah, good," Ray replied. He looked at his watch. As Frankie was closing the blinds of the store so that they would not have anyone looking in, Ray became very aware of the fact he was alone in a room with Frankie. He became very aware of the fact that the previous fact made him immensely uncomfortable.

"So, uh. Where are the, uh, um, girls?" Ray didn't want to sound too eager. He WAS eager, of course, but not so much because he was really anxious to see the girls and get started. No, he was eager to have the room be filled with bodies that were neither his nor Frankie's.

"Oh, they will be arriving here at any second. You know women, they take a long time to do anything! They are always late!"

"Right," Ray grunted. And then he realized something. Sometimes a fact can be staring a person right in the face. It could be something totally within your grasp that you should understand immediately. Usually, it is just a detail set within a set of facts you have glossed over. Frankie had been talking about them both getting their dicks sucked, and he may very well have meant it. Either that, or male "models" were on their way, too.

Ray wasn't sure which made him less comfortable. On the one hand, sex with random women under the camera was enough to make him so anxious he was already shaking. On the other hand, if the guys were coming in, they'd either be big jock types that would make him feel like shit, even in front of girls he didn't care about, or more Frankies, if that could be imagined. Neither one of these were pleasant.

"Uh, Frankie," he began, even less sure than usual as to how to proceed. "So, uh, what. The girls, they're, uh, they're with each other? Or what?" This was Ray at his most eloquent on the subject.

"Oh, you mean the clam-diving action? Yes, there will be some pussy-on-pussy action! You like that, eh, Ray?"

Ray wondered how the fuck he should answer that one and decided not to answer at all. "Any guys coming over?" Jesus, that felt stupid.

"Of course, Ray Brautigan my boy! You and I can not fuck these girls all night by ourselves! We are not professionals on all sorts of drug enhancements! Besides, men do not want to see guys like me fucking women. And girls may want to fuck you all the time, Ray my boy, but men do not want to watch you fuck girls. Not American men. You remind them too much of what they might be. They want to see meat with large cock fuck the girls. That is why I hire Steven."

Steven. *'Well,'* Ray thought, *'at least I don't have to get my dick dirty fucking whatever girls would agree to do this. Jesus, why would someone agree to be involved with this?'* Ray then remembered that he was involved with it because he needed money like crazy, and so, probably, did these girls, whoever they were.

To pass the time, Ray set up his tripod and camera. This was not a good way to pass the time, as it took only two minutes. Ray began wandering around the store, looking at the selection. Halfway through the "War" section, Frankie got a call.

His ring tone was "Strangers in the Night," oddly enough. Probably one of those assholes that romanticized the Rat Pack as something more than a talented bunch of singers of dubious moral fiber. Vegas was full of folks who were sure that things were so much better then, when the mob was in control and everyone knew it. Maybe it was. Ray, getting a light reading in the video store in which he was shooting illicit porn, was not one to argue about how things might be better.

"Yes, hello, this is Frankie. Oh, hello, darling sweetheart! Yes, that one. OK. Yes, I hear the car. I will let you in now. OK." Frankie put the phone away. "Here comes pussy!" he shouted to Ray. Ray looked intently at his camera, as if it could take him away from where he was.

When Frankie opened the door, Ray nervously shot a look at the people entering. Two girls and one guy. The guy had a shaved head and a goatee that was probably in style six years ago somewhere. He wore a black muscle shirt with an "extreme" barbed wire tattoo on his left forearm. He had two thick gold chains. Ray wondered if anyone had ever told this guy how gay he looked. It certainly wasn't going to be Ray.

One of the girls had a blonde dye job, an amount of make-up somewhere between Kabuki and evangelist, and the kind of body dumb guys thought was "curvy." That's probably what she would put on a personals ad, too. Or "bouncy." What they really mean is "fat." You'd see this girl in a strip club and know she wasn't there just making money to help her with college. She was a lifer, and had clearly moved on to bigger and worse things.

The other girl caught Ray's eye. She seemed to be of Latin descent. She had long brownish hair with blonde (this dye job seemed much more professional) highlights pulled back in a ponytail, a fair and creamy complexion, and slight freckles under her somewhat-almond-shaped eyes. Her lips were full and juicy and Ray realized he was staring.

This was the sort of girl he'd notice on the street. Anywhere. She wasn't the most beautiful woman in the world, but she was hot. She seemed to be in good shape, too. Ray couldn't figure it out. Why was she here? Why would a girl like that be involved in something this disgusting? Surely there were other ways to make money, though Ray didn't know exactly how much the girls were making. Or even how much he was making.

It was a good thing he never became an accountant, because he could never remember to ask things like that. It just seemed rude.

"Welcome, women and man! I am glad you could make it. This will be a good time for us all, I am sure. Cassandra, Sarah, and Steven, this is Ray Brautigan. He will be the photographer tonight. He is professional photographer with great art background!"

"Whatever, just don't stare at my dick, queer," Steven helpfully added.

Sarah, the fat one, gave him a look. "I ain't fuckin him for free, you know."

"Do not be rude, Sarah!" Frankie replied. Ray didn't think it would do much good. He bit his own tongue, knowing that giving his opinion on the idea of fucking that cow would not help the evening in the slightest.

Cassandra walked up to Ray. "Do you like Ansel Adams?" she said, seemingly out of nowhere. Ray was taken aback. He'd done a term paper on Adams, but honestly couldn't remember the last time he'd heard the name.

"Uh, yeah, actually. You?"

Cassandra nodded. "Listen, I'm not really here with these two, so please don't think I'm an idiot or something. I dance with Sarah and this side job is great money. I'm probably talking too much here, but you have no idea how glad I am to see someone who isn't these three," she said quietly. "So, listen, I'm begging you here, Ray. Don't be creepy. Be someone I can talk to in between shoots and not stare at my tits or something, OK?"

Ray slowly nodded his head. "Yeah. Uh, I feel weird about doing this, too, but I could really use the money."

"No kidding. So you're a professional photographer? Have I seen your work?"

"Probably not, actually," Ray said. "I, uh, I had some gallery shows years ago. I haven't, uh, had that kind of work in a long time."

"So you shoot porn? I used to kid my friend around, he went to film school. I always said he was going to end up shooting porn. Does that really happen?"

Ray shrugged. "I actually, uh, I do private investigation work. So I shoot that sort of thing." Ray had a quick flash of memory. "Wait, you're not in high school are you?"

Cassandra laughed. "Oh, hell, no. But thanks, I guess. Weird question."

"Oh, I, uh, I had this client, a girl, and she ended up being a high school, uh, kid. It was weird."

"Did you sleep with her?" Cassandra asked.

"No! Jesus, no! I—"

"Hello, love birds over there! You can talk about each other's genitals later! We have fucking to do!" Frankie was a master of words. At that moment, Ray wanted to be a master of not being where he was.

He wasn't, though.

"Talk to you later. Don't be creepy," Cassandra repeated. Ray nodded and actually felt marginally more at ease.

# CHAPTER ELEVEN

"OK, boys and girls and men and women," Frankie began, "first we shoot the girls looking at videos and of course they get so turned on they fuck each other! Get into your costumes, everyone."

Frankie handed Steven a duffel bag. Steven took out a blue polo shirt and khaki pants. "What the fuck? I'll look like a dork."

"Goddammit, Steven! You will look like video clerk! They are your customers and they fuck in your store then you fuck them! People all around will jerk off to this! Jesus Christ! You are the cock, I am the brain. You put on the clothes so you can take them off later."

Ray had to stifle a snicker. Frankie unleashed on someone he didn't like wasn't so bad, it would seem. As everyone changed Ray wasn't sure where to look. In a strip club you're supposed to look at the girls. At home, you can look at girls who might actually sleep with you. But in this situation he'd had no previous experience. He didn't want to look at Sarah or Steven, so that was out. He knew that he wanted to look at Cassandra, but didn't want to be creepy. What would be creepier, looking or looking away? Ray couldn't decide, so he pretended to be fixing something with his camera.

He did notice that Steven did end up looking pretty much like a video store clerk. Maybe at a gay porn rental place, but, hey, he was close. The girls, however, lacked this feeling of verisimilitude. Ray could not rule out the possibility that hookers from the future might come back in time to rent videos, though he had never seen this happen himself in real life.

Sarah looked completely ridiculous in some sort of pleather bikini/skirt combination, replete with cheetah spots. Ray made a mental note to ask Frankie who had decided upon that particular look.

Cassandra's outfit was slightly less insane and, to her credit, she almost pulled it off. Almost. It was a red tube top with some kind of mesh thing underneath covering her arms and an extremely tiny black skirt. Cassandra caught him looking and she gave a bemused shrug. Ray smiled and picked up his tripod, moving it to the area where Frankie was talking to the girls.

"OK, so you look at these romantical comedies and it makes your pussies wet, OK? Then you start going at it! Ray here, my boy, will shoot you with his camera. You sure you do not need more make-up, Cassandra?"

She shot a quick look at Sarah's face, a quick look to Ray, and back to Frankie. "Uh, no."

"Oh, you are going for the 'barely legal' hot fuck babe look, I see, very smart!"

"Uh, yeah," she replied, shooting another look to Ray. Ray again suppressed his laughter. This wasn't going to be so bad after all. Frankie moved out of the shot and the girls posed as if they were looking through the racks. Ray shot a couple of pictures and they continued. Sarah didn't seem to know what to do, but Cassandra picked up a title and pointed. Ray chuckled as she started acting as though she were turned on by the very thought of Hugh Grant or Tom Hanks or whoever it was. She began touching herself and Sarah, now understanding, followed suit. Ray shot picture after picture while Frankie commented from behind.

"Good work, ladies! Oh, your pussy juices, they flow now! You want fuck action! Ray, take the pictures, show them wanting the fuck action!"

As the girls started awkwardly making out, Ray realized he had a bad angle. "Hold on, let me take it off the tripod," he said.

"Oh, listen to my boy Ray! He is such a good picture taker he takes off the tripod! This will be super hot fuck action tonight!"

Ray rolled his eyes and loosened his camera. "OK, ready," he said. The girls started kissing again as he moved around for various close-ups. Sadly enough, this was much closer to actual photo work than he'd been able to do in ages. He lost track of the subject matter and just started taking the photos.

It felt good.

He didn't really even notice when the girls had removed most of their clothing and were mouth and finger fucking each other. He didn't notice what Sarah did to herself with the video case, but he got the shot. Ray was in the zone, and it was a zone he hadn't been in since Everything Went To Shit. There wasn't thinking, judging, worrying, just taking pictures. He finished off two rolls of film without even pausing.

"OK, OK, that was the good clam-smack action but we need the fuck!" Frankie announced. As Ray reloaded, Steven came over and Frankie described his, well, vision for the shoot. It was clear that Frankie actually took some pride in this stuff and wanted his basement porn to be the best basement porn you could find. It was almost respectable.

When Ray was fully reloaded, he tried his damnedest to get back into that zone, but Steven's abrasive presence made it difficult. Ray shot them undoing his pants and retrieving his admittedly huge wang. Sarah started working on it and Ray got some good close-ups, starting to ignore what exactly he was shooting again.

"Hey, queer, I said don't stare at my dick!" Steven called out.

Like someone still half-asleep, Ray couldn't figure out what that meant. "Wha?"

"You're staring at my dick, you fag!"

Ray thought for a moment. "I'm the photographer. I'm taking pictures. I have to look to take pictures."

"Stop enjoying it, though! I know you want me to fuck you!" Steven replied.

Ray gave up on finding reason within Steven and turned to Frankie. "What the fuck is he talking about Frankie?"

Frankie shrugged. "Steven always thinks the photographers want him to fuck them in their asses. I don't question it too much, he has big cock and works cheap."

"I know you want me, fag!" Steven repeated.

"No, I really fucking don't, Steven. You fucking gross me out."

"So you admit you're a fag!"

Frankie interrupted. "Ray Brautigan is not a homosexual. Ray Brautigan fucks only the finest of bitches, and they surround him like flies on shit! And those women are not even paid to fuck him, Steven! When was last free pussy you got? Now shut the fuck up and make the porn fuck action or I find new big dick asshole!"

This seemed to shut Steven up. Cassandra was giving Ray a weird look, somewhere between dubious and amused. It was Ray's turn to shrug. The shoot went on as planned, with Sarah and Steven fucking in all the requisite positions. When Cassandra re-entered the shot, she was totally nude and Ray noticed a tattoo at the base of her spine. He only noticed it because it wasn't one of the five tattoos that every dumb sorority/sorority-wannabe girl gets. It was a star with an anarchy-style "A" inscribed within it. He made sure to get a shot of it and moved along.

It was now impossible to zone out. Ray couldn't deny that he found Cassandra attractive. Seeing her blowing and fucking and contorting with these two disgusting pieces of flesh bothered him in some intrinsic way.

"Gotta reload," Ray mumbled. Cassandra immediately stood up while Sarah and Steven seemed not to hear him.

"So you only fuck the finest of bitches?" Cassandra asked. Ray dropped his film.

"Uh, don't mind, uh, Frankie. You know how he is. He sees me with some, uh, pretty girls and so he assumes I'm, you know, uh, sleeping with them."

"Right," she laughed. "At least he can tell you're a better guy than this freak. Even with the condom I'm pretty sure I need to bathe for the rest of the week."

Ray laughed and picked his film back up and started loading it. "So, uh, why did you . . ."

"Money, Ray. Probably the same reason as you, unless you actually do like staring at gross big dicks."

"Steven, you keep fucking and come before that camera is loaded, it'll be the last time you come in this country, you fuck brain!" Frankie yelled.

"I'm ready," Ray said, and back to work they went. Steven and Sarah seemed oblivious to the rest of the room and Cassandra seemed at a loss for something to do. She picked up a random movie and gave a big thumbs up smile to the camera.

"That is very funny but you cannot come when you laugh!" Frankie said, laughing. "Make with hot fuck action! Maybe you need your own dick? Ray, you get in there! I will take hot fuck pics! I will leave out your face so all your beautiful women do not see you in porn film fucking another beautiful woman!"

"Uh, urrr," once again, Ray had no answer for Frankie. He was actually getting an erection at the thought.

"Uh, wait," Cassandra said. "What if I fingered myself while, uh, playing with her boobs?" Frankie's eyes lit up like an octogenarian's birthday cake.

"Very good! You be director one day!" he shouted. Cassandra went to work as promised and Ray continued shooting. He felt relieved; this wasn't the sort of way he should be with a girl. He couldn't help feel a bit rejected, though. Cassandra seemed cool. But the thought of sucking his dick was apparently less appealing than what she was doing already.

Ray remembered he was some random guy with a beat up face taking pictures of her fucking and figured she made the right decision. Ray was about to finish the roll when Steven finished on Sarah's face. He immediately started to pack up, wanting to get out as fast as he could. It was going on nine and he just wanted to see his friend play.

"Good work, good work, everyone. This was great fuck shoot! We will all see much money from this, I guarantee. No! Sarah, do not use Robin Williams movie to wipe your face. Use your own goddam shirt! Jesus Christ, show respect!"

Ray was almost finished dismantling his tripod and camera. "I'll get these developed and I'll call you, Frankie. Can I get, uh, paid now?"

"Oh, you are leaving? This is too bad, Ray. It is fun fuck time, not business fuck time!" Everyone looked at Frankie reaching in his pocket, disgusted. When he pulled out a pack of coke, some faces changed. Ray shook his head.

"I, uh, I gotta go."

"The old balls and chains is getting you, eh? Oh, Ray, my boy, what will we do?" Frankie pulled out an impressive stack of twenties. "Eight hundred," he whispered in Ray's ear. "You hide this, my boy." Ray pocketed the money and nodded.

He thought about saying goodbye to Cassandra, but figured that would be creepy. He just gave a general wave to everyone and walked out the door, broken down camera in a backpack. '*Just as well*,' he thought to himself. '*She probably has issues*.' He took the money out and split it up between several pockets, even in his shoe. If he got mugged this time, they wouldn't get everything. He mentally oriented himself, trying to figure the cheapest and fastest way to get to Stinky's.

"What, you're going to leave me in there?" he heard. It was Cassandra, back in a T-shirt and jeans. "Jesus, even if I liked coke, that wouldn't be enough . . ."

"Oh, uh, sorry. I just, you know. I had to go."

"Right," she said. "I gathered that. If we end up doing this again, please don't leave me alone with those creepos."

"Yeah, OK. No problem." Ray felt like he needed to apologize, but he wasn't sure why. "Well, I have to go."

"Yeah, I know. You drive here?"

Ray shook his head. "Frankie did. Car ride from hell."

Cassandra laughed. "Well, I had both Steven and Sarah to deal with. His car smelled like farts mixed with asparagus. I wanted to puke."

Ray chuckled and wondered what he was supposed to say.

"It's weird, isn't it?" she asked.

"What?" Ray was genuinely confused.

"This. Trying to talk after, you know, what we just did. It's like talking to someone after a drunken one night stand. Except we didn't do anything. Well, you didn't."

Ray nodded. The need to apologize came back. "Sorry, uh, about that."

"Don't worry," she said. "I wasn't offended. I'd definitely rather fuck you than that guy, but I could tell you were freaked out."

Ray felt like a giant crazy pussy at this point. "I wasn't freaked out. I, uh, just . . ." but deep down he knew that he was lying.

"Right, Ray," Cassandra laughed. "I would be, too. Don't worry about it. So, uh, where you going? Want to share a cab west?"

"Uh, going east actually. But thanks. I usually just take the bus."

"Environmentalist, huh?" she asked with an eyebrow arched.

"Huh? Oh. No. Just poor."

"See you around, Ray," she said.

Ray looked at her as he started walking. She was really cute. "OK. Bye, Cassandra." But there was no way to go from here to anything else. Besides, he had to find Jenny. And get rid of the kid. It was odd: he was having more girl problems now than in that long-distant past when he was still getting some.

"It's Cass," she said, but Ray probably didn't hear her.

# CHAPTER TWELVE

At the bus stop, Ray fought the urge to call Jenny. Ogami would maybe have better luck, and they'd probably just end up seeing her tomorrow. Besides, Ray really dreaded explaining Amy to Jenny. He'd spend the rest of his life living that one down. Today's job and Cassandra would probably stay under wraps, too. Just something wrong about it.

So he sat and waited in the back of the bus, ignoring the other degenerates and wondering if they'd notice if he took out his flask. When he saw that two other guys were already hitting it, he decided to quietly join them. If nothing else, the stench of the bourbon overpowered the body odor of the other passengers. If nothing else part two, it made the ride seem faster.

Ray pocketed the flask as he stepped out of the bus. In a few blocks, he'd be there. He was excited to see Ogami's band again. It usually lead to a fun night. But he couldn't shake feeling anxious about Amy coming. How could she not be trouble?

As he walked, he remembered the 800 dollars he was carrying. It was pretty good pay for the amount of work he'd done, but it still wasn't quite what was stolen before. He quickly got paranoid, worried that someone would rob him and beat him up again. He nervously looked at the people around him and walked a bit faster. Then, he realized that if he were drinking, no one would think he'd have that kind of money. Unless they just thought he had to have something and that a drunk would be easier to mug. He hesitantly took a sip just to calm himself.

It was five after ten when he got to Stinky's. He hated being late. It made him more nervous than anything else. And he wasn't really even late, technically. O wouldn't go on for another fifty-five minutes at least. But being late when meeting someone was just unacceptable. He quickly paid the cover and went in.

He then remembered that no matter how late he felt, he was never as late as the girl he was meeting. It was a law of the universe. He briefly questioned what happens to lesbians, but decided to take a seat at the bar first. He put his coat on another, grudgingly remembering that he was supposed to save it.

Some punkass girl bartender took his beer order. Ray wondered why people would bother putting that shit in their nose and lips. Was it attractive to someone? It looked gross and painful. He tried to picture the girl without all the metal. Without it she was probably completely unremarkable. Like himself. Well, she stood out now. Congratulations were in order.

He remembered when he and Jenny had dressed up as ninjas and gone to a local Goth club. Some of the folks seemed to enjoy it, some even seemed in on the joke, but generally the night was ridiculously dressed people laughing at ridiculously dressed people. Everyone wants to feel better than someone. Ray had Frankie for that.

He ignored the opening act, not quite in the mood for acoustic comedy duos. He craned his neck around to see if Ogami was out, but didn't see him. Ray figured he was back stage getting ready. Soph, too, probably.

So, he sat and he drank. He looked at his watch and it was fifteen after ten. This was officially late, even by feminine standards. He thought that maybe she'd decided not to come and couldn't tell if he were relieved or disappointed. Less hassle, even if she was fun. Or, perhaps, she'd been stopped at the door. But Ray knew that last one was unlikely. No power in the universe could turn that girl away.

He found himself turning whenever he heard the door open, and silently cursed himself for it. He didn't know if he was looking for O, Jenny, Soph, or even Amy, but he felt creepy and desperate no matter who it was. He ordered three fingers of stiff, good bourbon and decided to concentrate on that, instead.

It was good and smooth, and had an aftertaste with a hint of vanilla and caramel. It was gone before he knew it and he'd ordered another. He felt a familiar slap on the ass. "Hey, HomO," he said, turning. But it wasn't Ogami, it was Amy. "Oops."

"Oh, man, boys are weird," she said. "What's that?" She took his glass and took a long pull. She winced a bit, and made a slight cough. "Holy shit," she said. "That's not scotch."

"Uh, no, it's bourbon. It's good, though," he felt defensive for some reason.

She nodded. "Fuck yeah it is!" She took another sip and looked stageward. "Those cuties your friends?"

"No. That's the opening act. Ogami's on next. Wait, you really think those guys are cute?" Ray was astounded. They weren't that much better looking than he was. A simple shrug was her only answer.

"So what'd you do today?" she asked.

"Uh, just some photography," Ray dodged.

"Yeah? Anything cool?"

"No." Ray had to end this inquiry fast. "What about you? Oh, that's right, school. Don't you have homework?"

"No, I skipped today, har har har. I broke up with Tom and needed a day to be me by myself."

"Oh. He go to the same high school as you?"

"Not quite. I met him at his video store." Ray felt his cheeks redden. "He's too old for high school, anyway. He's, like, your age, probably. Thirty-six."

"Jesus!" Ray spat. "He's older than me! How could you date someone that old?"

"Not a very consoling friend, are you Ray? I dunno, sometimes you date people you shouldn't. No big deal. He was fun for a while and had good taste in music."

"But, I mean, you're so young!"

"Get over it. Not everyone ages the same way. Most girls my age shouldn't date someone in their thirties, I know. But I'm not most girls. I'm Amy Gordon, dammit."

Her force of personality left Ray little choice but to drop the subject.

"So, anyway, how are you?" she asked.

"What? I'm, uh, OK."

"No, dumbass. That's what you're supposed to ask. You're my friend and I've gone through a break up! Jesus, Ray, step lively here!" Amy turned to the punky bartender and ordered "What he's having."

"Oh. So, anyway, how are you?"

Amy took a drink. "Eh, I'm OK. Trying to decide if I want to 'get back out there' or just hang out with myself. Know any cute single guys?"

Ray almost pondered the question. "No," he said with only a moment's hesitation.

"That's too bad. And here you are, but you said we're not allowed to fuck, and that's kind of a deal-breaker for me, if you understand."

Ray shook his head, thinking he was beginning to get her sense of humor. "Ray Brautigan," he said, bourbon flowing through him, "is like an entry-level secretarial position. You've got to have a high school diploma or equivalent to get me."

Amy stopped for a moment, mid-drink, and stared at Ray. "Well, I'll be damned! There's the fun Ray! I was afraid you got pod-personed. Relax. This isn't some Russian novel and I'm not going to lead your life down a trail of pain and misery. We're two friends who like to have fun. OK?"

Against the better judgment he didn't actually have, Ray relented. "Yeah, OK. That sounds fun. But hands off my pecker!"

Amy laughed. "I'll try, but I make no promises. Here's to it," she said, raising her glass.

Ray clinked it. "It's OK with me," he said. They downed another big glass a piece and Action Friend Force left the stage at some point. They moved from the bar, new drinks in hand, ready for the coming onslaught of sound. The Man in Black blared over the sound system and they sang about cocaine blues together. Then they sang about feeling the noize together. Then the sound system went blank for a second.

"Ladies and gentlemen, drop your pants for THE LOOOONE WOOOOOLVES!" the DJ announced. Ray and Amy cheered like lunatics as Ogami and his band took the stage. Scott came out first and sat behind the drums. Julio on bass. Shithead on lead. Ogami came out last, guitar held cockily at an angle. He looked at the band, and looked out in the audience.

"Hey, yo," he called out. "We're the Lone Wolves. We're here to rock and get you all laid. Thank us later. Here we go!" He counted off and they ripped into a hard, fast song about booze.

Ray remembered when Ogami wrote this song, they were out together at the Hole and Ogami had been inspired to write a country tune in the style of Merle Haggard. His band, of course, didn't play that sort of music, so when he brought it to them it got sped up, distorted, and thoroughly rock-ified.

Ogami was on and the band was with him. The audience was into it, dancing and hollering the whole set through. Cheers erupted for a cover of the theme from "Never-ending Story." The new songs seemed to work well (especially "(The Smell of) Your Taint") and the older songs definitely seemed recognized. It dawned on Ray that the band was at the point where they had fans. His friend had fans.

This was very strange.

They also covered "Earth Angel," nice and slow. After cheers of recognition, the various folks in the audience actually started pairing up like it was prom, dancing awkwardly from side to side. Ray stood there, somewhere between shock and awe, watching rough rock and rollers and indie scenesters get their high school on.

"Ray!" Amy cleared her throat. "I am SO not letting you make me just stand here like an idiot! Come here!" She grabbed him and pulled him to her.

"Uh, er," he stammered.

"Jesus. I promise that I am not going to fuck you here on this dance floor. Shut up and dance with me, dork."

Ray complied, of course, and they joined the other stilted back-and-forth-ers. Ray tried not to notice that apple smell in her hair again.

"So, you want to be my date to the prom?" Amy asked.

Ray didn't let go, but he stiffened. "Um, I don't think—"

"I'm just kidding, doofus. I'm not even going to the dumb thing. God, I've never met a boy so afraid of girls, and that includes Jason Smith in kindergarten. What did we ever do to you?"

The question was unexpected, and Ray tried to find an answer. Nothing came to mind. He'd had girlfriends and affairs, and none of them had gone particularly horribly. Just the same old bullshit, really. Why WAS he nervous?

"Nothing, really," he answered at last. "Guess I just never know where I stand," he said unwittingly. Where had that come from? This nice bourbon was talkative. "Or whatever," the non-bourbon part of him quickly added.

"Jesus," she added, head on his chest. "Your heart! You OK?"

"Uh, yeah. It's always a little fast. You know, dancing, and drinking and shit."

"Anyway, I like your T-shirt. It's soft." She rubbed her cheek on it.

He tried harder not to notice the apple smell. "That's, uh, because it's real old. Almost as old as you, I guess."

"Awesome!" she said as they danced. The song trailed off and the band walked off stage. People started cheering for an encore, and Ogami walked immediately right back on.

"I hate pretending like I'm not going to come right back out here. We're wasting valuable rocking time! Come on!" The rest of the band joined him, Scott counted off, and they absolutely RIPPED through "Sword of Vengeance," like their cocks depended on it. Ray found himself screaming and whooping the whole way through, caught up in the pure magic fuck of rock and roll.

Afterwards, to much applause, the band actually left the stage for real and the house lights came up just a bit.

"Hey, thanks," Amy said. "These guys rock. Want another bourbon?"

Ray nodded. "Yeah, but I gotta go see a man about a horse."

"No problem, this one's on me, dork." Amy went towards the bar while Ray went to the men's room. The men's room at Stinky's made Ray's dirty asshole look like an OCD sufferer's dining room table. He tiptoed in, careful not to put his entire foot down on anything, just in case. This was not an easy task after a handful of bourbons.

The difficulty increased exponentially when you took into account that no unsuicidal person would ever actually touch anything in the bathroom with his bare hands. So if you started to fall, you used your elbows against a wall to balance you. At a younger age, Ray saw it as a rite of passage. These days, it was an annoying routine, like most anything else. Tip-toes, elbow-balanced drunk pissing. Ray was happy he didn't even splash himself any.

It was set to be a fun night. Ogami would be pumped from the show. They'd all go out and have a party, and Ray could even buy a few rounds. It was starting to feel like old times.

But it wasn't old times. Jenny wasn't there, a seventeen year old girl was. Ray tiptoed back out of the bathroom and wiped his toes on the mat outside the room. He started back to the bar, looking for Amy. Some oaf with a ponytail was chatting her up. Ray's first impulse, after feeling heat on his cheeks, was to let her talk to the guy.

He always tried to let Jenny chat up whoever she wanted to; they were friends, after all, and no one likes a cock-blocker.

But, again, this wasn't Jenny. This was a seventeen year old girl, and some fucker with a dumb haircut wasn't about to be doing anything she'd regret. Ray walked right on up. "Hey, Amy," he said.

"Amy?" Ponytail said. "I thought you said your name was Amanda."

"Uh," Ray said.

"Um, yeah, but my boyfriend Ray calls me Amy. It's an old joke," Amy replied.

Amy might as well have said "Um, yeah, but my boyfriend zinga zunga plee dowkly," the way Ponytail lost interest when he heard "boyfriend."

"Yeah, OK, see you around," he said, absent-mindedly and left. Amy cracked up immediately.

"Amanda?" Ray asked.

"I dunno, it was the first thing that came to my head. I didn't want some long-haired loser knowing my real name. Ick!"

"Good thing your boyfriend was around, huh?" Ray said.

"Yeah, yeah, shut up. Here's your goddam bourbon," she said. "Which one is your friend?"

"The lead guy. Ogami. He'll be out in a bit, his girlfriend, too. You, uh," Ray hesitated, but things felt nice. "You want to come out with us afterwards?"

"Let's see, I could go have fun with my friend Ray or I could stand here and swat away creeps all night. Hmmmm. This is a tough one, give me some time." She winked and drank a big gulp of bourbon. Ray found no good reason not to do the same himself.

"Hello, Ray," a familiar Brazilian voice said. Ray turned around to see Soph. He put his hand out for a handshake, but she'd have none of that. The two cheek kiss that even bourbon couldn't make comfortable. "And who is this?"

"This is my friend Amy. Amy, this is Sophia, Ogami's girlfriend."

"Hi!" Amy waved.

"Ogami said to meet him in the back. He didn't want to walk through the crowd and waste any of his drinking time. Are you ready?"

Ray looked to Amy who downed the last of her drink. Ray did likewise and answered, "Yeah, let's do it."

As Ray was throwing down a couple more bucks for an extra tip, he noticed Amy do likewise. When you spend enough time in bars, you notice the tippers. They're the type you want to know. Not because they'll buy you drinks (they will), but because even in a lousy life lived in dank, dark holes that smell of vomit and stale beer, it's good to know who the decent types are. And it's a rule that you treat the service well, period.

Ray and the two girls ducked out through the exit and Ray lit a cigarette in the night air. "Where's O?" he asked after a satisfied exhale.

Sophia shrugged. Then a car honked a familiar honk. That old black Mustang was revving up. The trio trotted over. "Good show, man," Ray said.

"Thanks. You must be Amy, huh? Good to meet you." O could be very charming when he needed to. "Now climb the fuck in so we can get stupid!"

Ray opened the passenger door and let Amy in the back seat first. He climbed back there next, cramped like a woman on the rag. Soph got in the passenger seat and they were off.

"Where are your band mates?" Soph asked.

"Johnny's girlfriend's birthday, so he had to skedaddle over to her place. Scott had to study. And Julio might meet us later. You know him."

When Ray noticed only Amy didn't laugh, he explained, "Julio claims to live on Mexican time. He shows up where he wants, when he wants. For anyone else, it would be infuriating. But with him, it's just kind of, you know, annoying-but-cute."

"Like you?" Amy asked. Ray turned a brighter red than he could imagine.

"Ha! Exactly! I owe you a drink, girl!" Ogami said. "So, the Hole?"

"Yeah, I like that place," Amy answered for everyone.

"It's OK with me," Ray said.

"I take it I'm driving tonight?" Sophia asked. "Just as well, I have to do a show tomorrow. Trapeze with hangover? Do not try this."

"Whoa, you're a trapeze girl?" Amy asked, eyes wide.

"Yes. Ever since I was a little girl." Soph turned around to get a better look at Amy. She was always big on eye contact. Ray couldn't ever figure out if it were a Brazilian thing or a privilege of being beautiful thing. "My family and I traveled all the way to Rio to see a circus when I was only two. I saw the trapeze girls fly through the air and they were so beautiful and wonderful it was like Superman was a princess. And I knew then that's what I wanted to be."

"That's my girl, Princess Superman," O interjected.

"That's awesome," Amy said. "That's so hot."

"Thank you! Ray, I like your friend! Keep her, OK? Oh, Ray, are you feeling fine? You look flushed." Soph reached back to feel Ray's forehead but he dodged her.

"Uh, I'm fine. Just a little warm in here, you know?"

"I know what this car needs. We need to roll," Ogami said. He rolled the windows down, turned the radio on and up, and blasted NPR from his stereo. "Awwww, yeah! Prairie Home in the hizzy! Fuck yeah!"

The rest of the car cracked up, slapping knees and all, as nearby pedestrians craned their heads, wondering if they heard what they thought they heard.

They blasted Garrison Keillor all the way to the bar, and, surprisingly, the joke never got old. Even to a degenerate, that soothing voice had its appeal. And Ray couldn't help but feel a little too postmodern when the "Guy Noir, Private Detective" bit was on.

# CHAPTER THIRTEEN

As soon as they walked in, Ogami made sure they all knew the first round was on him. "What're you having?" he asked.

"Gin and tonic," Sophia said. "Just the one, I'm driving."

"Scotch neat," Amy replied. Ogami nodded, duly impressed.

"Bourbon with a beer back," Ray said. He and the girls found a suitable booth, one they'd actually spent many at night at before with Jenny.

"So, Amy, what do you do?" Soph asked. "I know, it is a very boring question, but we can get it out of the way and then talk about the good things in life."

Ray's eyes darted around. He had known that the subject of Amy's age would eventually come up, but he had hoped it would at least be later. "Um," he said, trying to think of a way to stop this from happening.

"I'm a student," Amy said. "I used to work in a video store part time," she added.

"Oh? Where do you study? UNLV?"

Ray could feel the sweat on his back.

"No, at Las Vegas High School," Amy said. "I'm 17. But I'm thinking about going to UNLV."

Ray was sure he could hear his own heartbeat, Amy's, Soph's, and everyone else's in the bar. It felt like slow motion and he wanted like hell to have his drink in hand. Where was Ogami?

Amy continued, "Can you tell Ray's embarrassed to have a friend my age?"

"Oh, Ray!" Soph laughed. "You think I will judge you? When I was her age I had a boyfriend older than you! American men only worry about the things they shouldn't worry about."

"Uh heh," Ray laughed nervously. "Yeah, I know. It's not like we're even, uh, dating or whatever. I need all the friends I can get, anyway."

"I'll say, Jesus!" Ogami said, handing out drinks. "You need more friends just to carry your goddam drinks!"

"Hey, I got you back tonight, I got some money!" Ray said.

"Oh, you got that money back?" Ogami asked.

"Uh, no, new job. Here's to rock and roll," Ray raised his glass. The table clinked together and so began the night's real festivities.

Ray was happily surprised with how well Amy fit in to his circle of friends. He was always anxious about any intermingling of friends, much more so when one was an underage former client.

"Who's up for some Buck Hunter?" Ogami asked.

"Fuck yeah," Ray replied.

"Anyone else?"

The girls shook their heads. "You boys have your video game fun," Soph said. They giggled, they actually giggled. Ray shook his head as he and Ogami walked over to the video game in the corner. Ogami put two quarters in and grabbed the plastic shotgun.

"She's cool," he said.

"Yeah. Amy's all right."

"I think she likes you," he said while firing at something.

"What? What the fuck? No way. No."

"I dunno, maybe. Dude, why else would she be putting up with all of us? Oooh, missed it."

"Because you guys are fun and interesting and cool and shit."

"Hm, good point. YES! Got him! But, uh, why would she put up with hanging out with you if she didn't like you?"

"That's some fucked up logic, O."

"That's Zen, motherfucker. Here, your turn." Ogami handed the gun off to Ray. Ray took aim and waited. "Dude, I wouldn't judge you if you did her. She's hot and she doesn't look her age at all. Is she legal?"

"Yuck! I mean, yeah, she's hot and everything, but don't you think it's a little, I dunno, sick? Fuck, I shot a doe. I mean, she so goddam young. It'd be like taking advantage."

"Not every young girl is an innocent waif, man. You have to let them make their own choices. Don't shoot that doe."

"I'm not. Haha! Fuck you, buck! She just broke up with her boyfriend, she's probably just needing attention. That's taking advantage. Besides, no, I'm not. It's just wrong."

"Good shot," Ogami said. "Hey, it's up to you, clearly. I'm just saying I wouldn't think you were a creep or anything. As long as you don't bweak hew widdle heawt." Ogami's baby voice was not a very accurate one, but it was successfully annoying. "Seriously though, don't fuck her up even if you fuck her."

"I'm not going to fuck her! Goddammit, your turn."

Ogami took the shotgun. "Fine, fine. Dude, when was the last time you got laid, anyway?"

"It's been a while."

"What are you waiting for? Yes, got him!"

"I'm not waiting. I just haven't had the opportunity. I'm not a good looking baseball rock and roll star. I'm just me."

"Dude, you're a private dick! I know my dad got all kinds of tail before he finally married mom. It's like one of the few job perks."

"Not for this one, it isn't. Oooh, nice shot."

"Dude, I know why you're not getting any," Ogami said. "Goddammit! I totally fucking hit it! Bullshit! Your turn."

Ray struggled to finish gulping down his drink before taking the gun. "Why am I not getting any, oh wise Zen master? EAT SHIT BUCK! Because I suck?"

"Nope. Because of Jenny."

Ray concentrated on the screen in front of him, watching electronic animals run from tree to tree. "What?" he said, simply.

"You heard me. Jenny's the ultimate cock-blocker for you and you don't even know it."

Ray fired twice and missed. He was never good at video games. They seemed to be fun, always, but his inadequacy made them hard to enjoy. If Ray wanted to suck at something, he'd just stick with real life.

"What are you talking about? She hasn't even been around for months!" Ray holstered the gun. Game over.

Ogami smiled. "Hey, it's no biggie. Tell me, though. You ever compare girls to Jenny?"

Ray made a face. "No! Well, I mean, not like that. I mean, you compare everyone to everyone else, right? 'Oh, this person is more fun than that person,' whatever. It's not like, you know." Words.

Some people are gifted with tongues like shepherd dogs, corralling the words into their proper pens and routes. Ray's tongue was more of a spastic cat with digestive problems. "Not like that."

"OK," Ogami said. He always knew when to let shit go. "Hey, it's Julio!" he pointed towards the entrance. Julio gave them a slight wave and sauntered over.

"Hey," he said.

"How you doing?" Ray asked, as they shook hands.

"Hey, man, I'm cool. Just watched a TV show about lizards. Those fuckers are crazy."

"That's great, man," Ogami said. Julio's the guy who always got away with not having to make sense all the time. It just worked for him, like an ugly scarf on a cute, trendy girl.

They rejoined the ladies with Julio in tow. Introductions were made and Ray took a round of drink orders. Cliff was tending the bar, all business and a wry smile as usual. While arranging the drinks on a tray, he said, "Oh, hey. Shit, man, one of the other bartenders, a new girl, she said someone was in here a couple months ago looking for a white guy with glasses. She was all like, 'That's a lot of white guys,' and the girl said a name she didn't remember, of course, but that he was a private investigator. The new girl, Felicia, she thinks it's a joke and doesn't tell nobody for a while. But at her going away party the other night she mentions it. She couldn't remember anything other than she was cute and white. You know what she's talking about?"

Ray stared. "I really don't," he said.

"I'll keep an eye out," Cliff replied.

"Yeah," Ray mumbled. *'Fuck,'* he thought. *'What the shit does that mean? Maybe it was Jenny. Jesus, of all the nights not to be here. Who else would look for me? But Jenny knows where I live. Shit. What the fuck? Maybe a client? But they wouldn't know I came here. A cute girl. I don't know many cute girls. Jenny, Soph, Amy, that's pretty much it. Well, Cassandra was cute. But it couldn't have been her. What the fuck? Jesus, I hate this shit! How am I supposed to have fun tonight when all I can think about is this?'*

Ray realized he was still thinking quietly after sitting down and giving out the drinks. He also realized that he'd heard some thank-you's out there. "Uh, no problem," he mumbled, still lost in thought.

"What's wrong?" Amy asked. "You look weird."

Ray debated telling everyone, but figured it would feel good to get it off his chest. "It's just . . .it's weird. Cliff said a month or so ago some girl came in here looking for me. There was a new girl and she didn't take it seriously and he just found out. And now that new girl is gone, and she apparently didn't remember anything other than she was cute and white."

The table sat. "God, women just flock to you, Ray," Amy said. "How do you have any time to yourself?" The table laughed, including, reluctantly, Ray.

"It's hard, but they usually leave when I give them what they want."

"Oh, yeah? What's that? Cause you haven't given me shit!"

Ray had thought he was ready to joke with Amy about stuff like that. He was wronger than soy ice cream. Thankfully, the table's laughter excluded them noticing his embarrassment.

"Maybe it was that girl that used to come with you to our shows," Julio said. "Judy?"

"Jenny," Ogami corrected. Did he give Julio a look? It was difficult to tell.

"Maybe," Ray said.

"So when do I get to meet this Jenny? Everyone knows her but me!" Amy said.

"I dunno," Ray said. "She sometimes, uh, disappears for jobs or something. She still does photography for real."

"That's cool. Ray, you act like you're such a loser but all your friends are pretty awesome. Especially now that I'm one of them."

But Ray wasn't really listening. The din of the bar had gone from unspecific cacophony to every noise having its own annoying pitch and timbre. Another big slug of bourbon and it kind of flowed together. It was easy to put his friends' chatter in the same place as everything else, listening to different sounds. But he wasn't really listening, he was thinking. *'Why would whoever it was just come here and not call me? Dammit. What if it was something serious and they had no time or something? Or someone lost my number? Fuck. Jesus CHRIST!'* he thought. *'Who played all the goddam Springsteen?!'*

Everyone stopped and looked at him. Apparently, that last part wasn't a thought, it was out loud. "Yeah, man!" Julio joined in. "Fuck Jersey!" Soon enough, a juke box raiding party had been assembled. Dollar bills were their hand grenades and good music their mission. A rock and roll strike force, delta blues green berets. The party was started by an explosion of Mooney Suzuki.

*'Oh, Christ,'* Ray thought. *'I'm going to dance, aren't I?'* His fears were founded, as the whole table was soon flailing and jumping around like retarded heart attack victims on a trampoline. As Ray danced, mysterious women faded away. The shame of pornography was left behind. Clearly, all shame was gone. There was just the

music and the beat and the way the body felt loose and a part of everything all at once. It didn't matter who he was dancing with. It was erotic, but not sexual. Man, woman, friend, friend's girlfriend, dangerously young girl, weird Mexican, old smelly alcoholic that seemed to have joined them, it didn't goddam matter. When Amy rubbed against him, it didn't matter that she was young, that she was his friend, that Jenny wasn't there, anything. It just mattered that it felt right and good and fun and the three were synonymous right then and there.

The night flowed on and fatigue meant nothing. Booze was their energy now. Through some sort of boozosynthesis they nourished their bodies with drink after drink. Jesus Christ it felt so good. Everything was as it should be. Things were right.

# CHAPTER FOURTEEN

Ray would have woken up in an amazing mood if his stomach and head hadn't teamed up to fuck him over. He tried standing up but that didn't work too well. He was still dressed and something smelled funny. He had either had an intense wet dream or pissed himself. He reached a hand down and confirmed it was urine and not semen soaking his pants. His stomach then informed the rest of his body that the legs had to get moving immediately and he barely hobbled into the bathroom before the vomiting began.

Ray's head was swimming but he wasn't drunk enough for the vomiting to be a pleasant relief. His guts wretched and his throat burned. He choked, teared up, and gasped for air. The vomit was hot and acidic and in between bursts he'd try to spit the taste out to no avail. Ray cursed and wretched and his legs started to burn and cramp. He sat down on the cold damp floor, pants full of piss, hanging on to the toilet. He stared at the former contents of his stomach as if they held some clue, some message from on high.

If they did, the message was, "You drank too much, asshole."

The tears pooled in his glasses. He put them on the sink and wiped his eyes. He wanted to hit his head on the toilet until the pounding stopped. Every movement caused him pain. He rested his head on the toilet and didn't even try to reach the flusher.

At some later point he woke up with his head on the toilet. His headache was still awful, but more manageable. He found that with some difficulty he could even stand up. His vomit had been sitting in the toilet and the scent had filled the room. "Fuck," he said, lighting a match and flushing the toilet. "Fuck fuck fuck." He kept the match out and found an unfinished cigarette in his pocket. Aware that he might partially be smoking his own urine, he lit it anyway. He needed a cigarette bad.

"Fuuuuuuuuck," he repeated slowly. He massaged his temples while the cigarette dangled from his lips. His eyes were red as a union leader circa 1943. His ass-beating was barely noticeable in comparison. He thought back to the night and remembered the fun and grinned. He wasn't sure how he'd gotten home and had that sudden panic of "Shit, I hope I didn't do anything stupid." Ogami would be by later, and he was good at remembering the stupid shit that Ray had done.

He took a deep drag and took his pissy pants off and emptied his pockets. He hoped that the pissing had happened after he left everyone, but one never could be sure in times of heavy, heavy, stupid drinking. He finished the cigarette and the stripping and prayed to God the shower would actually have consistently hot water when he turned it on.

It did. For five minutes. Then the moaning and changing temperature began again. Ray didn't care. He tried to pretend it was some luxury sauna or spa thing. But his imagination wasn't that strong. He heard his phone ring in the next room, but he was too covered with soap and too filled with hangover to do anything about it. Ogami would leave a message.

He toweled off, again noticing the growing stink of his towel and sinkingly realized he would actually have to do laundry soon. This was the day he and Ogami would go to Jenny's house and see what she was up to. Ray took out his razor, remembered that he still didn't have any shaving cream. He soaped his face up as best he could and started shaving.

It hurt like fuck, but so did everything else at this point, so he just soldiered on. The shaving was not such a good idea. Beat up face, no shaving cream, hangover, sensitive skin to begin with. Ray saw no reason to stop making stupid mistakes, so he continued.

As he was rinsing, his phone rang again. He picked it up to make the loud noise stop. "Ray here," he said.

"Hey, bud, it's me." Ogami sounded chipper.

"Hey, you just call me?"

"Nope. Wasn't me. Hey, you still up for today?"

"Yeah," Ray said. "Yeah, sure. When you coming around?"

"How about one?"

Ray had no idea what time it was. "Uh, I dunno. What time is it?"

Ogami laughed on the other end. "Twelve-thirty, dude. Sounds like you've had an interesting morning. Anybody there with you?"

"No!" Ray looked around just to make sure. "No. Shit. I didn't do anything stupid, did I?"

"We'll talk in a half hour. Later, Gay."

"Later HomO."

Clean underwear, jeans without piss on them, and a new old ratty t-shirt and Ray was ready to go. His headache started throbbing harder so he popped some shady "pain pills" a client had given him and downed it with a small sip of bourbon. Hair of the dog was going to be put to the test yet again.

Ray also found his money stashes from throughout the previous night's clothing, and consolidated it under his futon next to the porn rags. He sighed when he saw them. Something less appealing about them now that he'd taken some photos himself.

Remembering, he took the rolls of film out of his briefcase and set them on his sink to remember to develop after visiting Jenny. He started to get excited and told himself she probably wasn't going to be around. He told himself this pretty strongly, almost enough to actually not make him anticipate it. Like when he was a kid, telling himself every Easter or Christmas morning, "Don't expect anything big. You may not get it and you don't want to be disappointed." But sometimes nothing could quell excitement.

There was the horn, and there went Ray out the door. When he climbed in the car he smelled it. "Eggs and bake-y, wakey-wakey!" Ogami gave handed him a Bacon McMuffin.

"Oh, shit! McDonald's breakfast. So awful and so delicious. Hey, how'd you get this at one?" Ray took a huge bite, grease battling it out with drugs, booze, and pain in his stomach.

"I know a girl," Ogami said. "Let's go see Jenny."

After he finished the McMuffin and orange juice, Ray finally asked. "So, seriously, I do anything I should know about last night?"

"Danced like a fiend, but that's pretty much it. Why, something worry you?"

"Heh. I, uh, I woke up with piss on my pants."

"Oh, shit! You fucking pissed yourself?!?" Ogami was doing the driving equivalent of doubling over with laughter. "Oh, fuck! When?"

"I have no idea. I guess while I was sleeping? Or on the ride home or something. I don't remember. Shit! Did Amy get home OK?"

"Yeah, we all got her a cab, don't worry. You should call her, she was fun."

"Yeah. So you're sure I didn't do anything, like, with her?"

"Oh, like that would be the end of the world. Get over it, Peepants."

"Shut up!"

"Ray pissed his pants!" Ogami sang, elementary school style. "Ray pissed his pants! Ray pissed his pants!"

Ray started to laugh but then felt his stomach. "Oh, shit. Maybe the McMuffin wasn't such a good idea . . ."

"You going to puke?"

"I don't think so. Feels like the runs. Again."

"Jesus, Ray. You're the worst diarrheaiac I've ever known. Fuckin' hold it in! Can you?"

"Yeah, it's not about to go yet. DefCon 3."

Ogami was the sort of friend with whom you could share intimate details of improper bowel movements. In fact, he might even be hurt if you didn't. That was a good sort of friend for Ray to have, because he had them often.

Ray took out a cigarette in hopes that it would magically cure his failing digestive system. "Smoke?" he asked Ogami. O nodded and took one.

"Shit, you still smoking these generic things? Fuck, they're nasty!"

Ray shrugged, waiting for the cigarette lighter to pop back out. "I dunno, you get used to them. Next time I'm gonna buy some good ones. Marlboros or Camels or even Dunhills."

"Yeah, you had a good job yesterday you said. What'd you do? Actual photography again?"

Ray paused to light his friend's cigarette and then his own. "Uh, kind of. For Frankie."

"Oh, Jesus. That little turd? What were you shooting? Was it . . .was it legal?"

Ray thought for a moment. "I don't know, actually. Probably not, but it wasn't anything like 'HOLY SHIT GET OUT OF HERE RIGHT NOW' illegal. Just porn in a video shop. Oh, get this!" Ray took a deep drag and felt his lungs ache. "We ended up shooting it at the video store where I was watching that Tom guy."

"Really? Tom, Amy's gay ex? That's fucking crazy. Whoa. That's nuts. Did you suggest it or something?"

"No," Ray said. "I think Frankie just knew the owner or manager or something. I actually saw Tom. It was fucking weird."

"Did you tell Amy?" Ogami asked casually.

Ray looked at him in shock. "Are you fucking kidding me? 'Hey, I ran into your gay ex at his video store because I was there shooting photographs for probably-illegal pornography.' I don't see that going over well anywhere, anytime."

"Why does it matter? You're 'just friends' or whatever, right? You'd never sleep with her, apparently, no matter how hot she is, or how hot she is FOR you."

"I dunno, that's not the sort of thing you tell a seventeen year old girl. It's sick and gross and whatever." Ray preferred not to think to heavily about certain parts of his life.

"She's not some vestal virgin, Ray," Ogami said, flicking a spent cigarette butt out the window. "Women are great, but you can't always treat them with kid gloves."

"I know!" Ray said automatically, refusing to examine whether it was true or not. "But she's seventeen!"

"So you can illegally drink with her, she can be sexually active, you can introduce her to all of us freaks, but she can't hear about you being involved in porn?" Ogami looked at Ray. Ray was always nervous when someone did this while driving. It made him very eager to please the person and get them to stop looking away from the road, even at a red light.

"Well, yeah. A lot of girls are grossed out by porn, or offended, or something."

Ogami turned back around and nodded. "True, yeah. She doesn't seem the type, but I guess you never know. Hey, what about the girls? Were they hot? Were they famous? Stupid questions."

"Yeah, they're not famous. Probably local strippers. One was this fat white cow. She was a gross bitch, I really didn't like her. The guy was a tool, too. I think he was closeted or something, the poor guy. But there was another girl, uh, Cassandra. She was actually kind of cute."

"Yeah? And you saw her naked?"

Ray laughed. "Yeah, I did. She was, yeah, she was hot. She seemed cool, too. We talked about photography and shit. She hated everyone else there, too."

"What was it like?" Ogami asked. "What was it like shooting a porno with a cute girl who talked to you? Were you all turned on or grossed out or what?"

Ray thought. Ogami always seemed to prevent him from avoiding thinking of the things Ray'd prefer to gloss over. Good friends don't just fit well together, they draw each other into larger spheres. "Well, sometimes it was just a job. But, uh, Frankie tried to get us to do something together."

"REALLY? Oh, fuck! On camera?"

Ray nodded. "Yeah. I mean, on the one hand, blowjob from hot girl, on the other . . .Jesus, you know? That's not how I want it to happen. Under Frankie's orders while he's snapping photos of it! That's fucking gross."

"Huh. Yeah, you always think that you'd love to be in a porno or something, but when you really think about what it would involve—I turn right here, right?"

Ray looked around. They were almost there. "Yeah." He kept re-reminding himself that she probably wasn't going to be there and there was nothing to be excited about. He wasn't listening to himself any more than he was to Ogami.

" —just freak you out. I can see that." Ogami had been speaking about something and Ray wasn't sure what. But he didn't seem to need to answer, so he just sat there.

They parked on the street and Ray's heart raced. He actually felt his mouth dry. He told himself he was being stupid, but that didn't change a goddam thing. They got out of the car and walked towards the loft.

"Don't get mugged this time," Ogami said. "I don't want to have to kill anyone today."

Ray gave a distracted laugh and quickened his pace. He stopped in front of the building. There was no sign of life, but knowing the folks that lived in the loft, it was still too early. They walked up to the door. And stood.

# CHAPTER FIFTEEN

"Uh, Ray, you gonna ring the bell?"

"Huh? Oh. Yeah." Ray rang the bell. There was no reply. He rang again. *'See, I knew she wouldn't be around.'* A crashing in an alley freaked Ray out, but it was probably just a cat or something.

Ogami put his finger on the buzzer and went to town on it. "WAKE UP!" he yelled at the inanimate machine.

"Shit! Stop it, man!" Ray said, not really knowing why. But if they didn't buzz too loud, he could always tell himself that, yeah, she was there and would have talked to him, but she was asleep. "Wait," he said. He listened closely and heard the tell-tale sounds of someone making their way down the three flights to the entrance. *'Oh Jesus Christ, she IS here,'* he thought.

A skinny white guy with thinning blonde hair opened the door in a sleepy stupor, wearing slippers, boxers, and a robe. "What the fuck?" he asked.

Ray didn't recognize him, but people tended to come and go. "Uh, is, uh, Jenny around? Jenny Meyer?"

The scrawny dude, even smaller than Ray, looked at him in dreamy confusion. "Uh, what? Who? Who the fuck's that?"

"Jenny Meyer. She lives here. We're her friends," Ray said, getting agitated.

"Uhhh, oh. I, uh, just moved in here. I don't know any Jenny, but that don't mean she's not here. Come on." The skinny guy led them inside and up the stairs.

"Uh, what's your name, dude?" Ogami asked.

"Michael. I'm Michael. What fucking time is it? I feel like shit."

"Uh, a little after one," Ray answered.

"Fuck, and it's Saturday, right?" Michael asked groggily.

"Yeah." There wasn't much else to say to him. They got to the actual entrance to the loft where everyone lived and he let them in.

"OK, well, I hope you find her or whatever. I'm going back to bed," Michael said and walked to his bedroom. Nyasha used to live in that room, Ray remembered. She had seemed pretty cool and always made these weird sculptures that reminded him of goblins.

"Uh, what now?" Ogami asked. "You know her bedroom, right?"

"Yeah. Should we go to it? Uh, what if," Ray's face got hot. "What if she's, uh, you know. With someone?"

"Jenny wouldn't give a shit. Come on, let's go surprise her."

They walked across the large common area and passed the library and the entertainment room. A couple of guys Ray didn't recognize were passed out in the latter. That wasn't very unusual, though. What was unusual was the smell. Usually Jenny got on everybody about making sure stuff was clean enough to smell OK. She had not done this recently.

When they got to Jenny's room they saw the door was no longer there, nor the curtains.

Nor much of anything else. Her file cabinet was there, but everything in it was gone. CDs, DVDs, photographs, mostly all gone. Random things laying around. A bean bag chair. A family photo from when she was young.

Her bed was gone.

"What the fuck?" Ray said out loud. "This is weird." He started looking around more closely. He opened desk drawers and found loose change and a pencil. None of her toys were there. A can of cat food sat on a dresser mostly empty of clothes. A t-shirt remained, with "Special Olympics" printed on it.

"Uh, should you be going through this?" Ogami asked.

"Um, I dunno. It's weird, though, right? Some stuff here, some stuff not. No bed."

"Um, man, I think she just moved and didn't take everything."

"Why not this picture of her family, though? Or this t-shirt? She loved this t-shirt." Ray was still holding both.

"I really don't know, man. But, uh, what else would be going on. Moved to another room?"

"Maybe," Ray said. He didn't stop looking around though. Almost everything was gone. Everything being gone would make sense. This didn't. This was weird. This looked hasty and forced. Something was wrong. He kept looking. He looked out the window where he'd looked in the night he was mugged. He could see where he was standing. He could see the wall behind him, where the thug must have been. He could see what was on that wall. A star was spraypainted large, with a big red anarchy "A" in the middle of it.

"Holy shit!" Ray said. "That graffiti! I've seen that! That was on that girl!"

Ogami was still in the doorway. "What?"

"Come here, that graffiti!" Ogami came over and Ray pointed it out. "That girl, Cassandra, she had that tattooed on her. What is that? Do you recognize it?"

"Uh, no," Ogami shook his head. "Never saw it before, I don't think. Or noticed it, at least. But, uh, isn't it right here, too?"

Ray jerked back, "Where?!"

Ogami was pointing towards the floor, where Jenny's bed once was. Carved into the hardwood was the same symbol. "Oh fuck! What the fuck? What's that mean?"

"I don't know," Ogami said. "She probably did both of them. Or a friend did. Could be an art thing we don't know about."

"What if it's something else?" Ray asked. "What if it means something? What if something happened?"

"Dude, I don't think anything happened. It's just a symbol."

Ray stormed out of the room, putting the picture in his pocket and holding the shirt still. "Hey! Jenny!" He yelled. "Jenny Meyer! Is Jenny here somewhere? HELLO?"

"Christ, keep it down, Ray, you're freaking me out," Ogami said.

"Something's wrong," Ray said.

"Who the fuck are you?" a rather large man said from another bedroom doorway. His girth was mostly by way of bodyfat, but six five and 250 lbs. is still a big motherfucker, no matter how you look at it. His eyebrows were bushy and black, his beard in need of a trim and a groom.

"Uh, I'm Ray. I'm a friend of Jenny's." Ray gave his "harmless puppy dog" smile. It rarely worked and usually just looked creepy and conniving.

"Jenny? There's no Jenny here."

"She, uh, lives here, or at least used to. How long have you been here?" Ray asked.

"I've been here fuck-you years. And eat shit-months. Oh, also, get-the-fuck-out-of-my-goddam-house weeks."

"Hey, now," Ogami said. "No need to get antsy. We're here visiting a friend."

"Like I said before, nobody with that name lives here. Now get the fuck out of here before I throw you out." He took a big, fat step forward.

Ray reflexively glanced at Ogami, whose body was tensing for a fight. "Listen, Fatfuck Ass-shit, calm the fuck down."

The big man looked at Ogami, perhaps sizing him up. Ogami didn't have the size, but he had the posture. The big 'un retreated back into his bedroom. Ogami watched him then gave Ray a look.

"Oh, yeah," he said. "Now, I think—"

He was interrupted by the big man coming back out with a goddam firearm in his hands.

"Jesus Christ!" Ray yelled at a higher pitch that he would have wished. Ogami just looked at it silently.

"OK, assholes. Here this is, break into my house again and I will fucking shoot you where you stand. Or sit. Or lay. Wherever you may be, I will shoot you. Now shut the fucking shit up and get the fucking shit out of my fucking apartment permanently."

Ogami looked to Ray who nodded his head. They walked out together, Ogami keeping an eye on the big man the entire time. Once they got to the door, the big man slammed it shut. They stood there for a minute and Ray saw the star/A symbol carved into the door, too. He pointed at it for Ogami to see but through the door they both heard, "I'm pretty sure this caliber will blow through this door." They moved along.

They didn't say a word until they reached Ogami's car. "Fucking asshole. Jesus. A fucking gun? Goddam piece of shit. Without that gun I could've—"

"Oh, it's cool, we're all right. But he's hiding something, that's for sure."

Ogami stopped and looked at his friend. "What are you talking about? He was a dick, but we were two strange guys in his apartment looking for someone he's never heard of."

"How could he have never heard of her? That's her place!"

Ogami sighed. "Not anymore, Ray. I think we've discovered why she hasn't called us or anything. She fucking moved, man. She's gone."

The car was silent as Ogami started the engine and pulled out. Ray looked out the window at the graffiti design. Right about where he got jumped. The same symbol on Jenny's door, on her floor under her bed, and on Cassandra's back. It had to mean something. That kind of shit isn't coincidence, it isn't happenstance. Too much.

"Something's wrong. I think something happened to her," he said quietly as they drove. "Why's that guy have a gun, anyway? Who has a gun?"

"People that live in the goddam ghetto have a gun, Ray. You got jumped here, he probably has to."

"Or he's the one who jumped me. Didn't want me looking into what was going on. Something happened that night. I saw something in Jenny's window. While I stood right there where the symbol is on the wall. This is something."

Ogami was quiet, but it wasn't a calm quiet. Ray knew his friend well enough to tell it was a seething quiet. These quiets never lasted long. Ogami wasn't Tupperware, he wasn't a good container. He was an exploder.

"Goddammit to hell, Ray! Fucking let it go! She fucking left! She didn't tell you! Or me! Or anyone! Friends sometimes aren't friends anymore, or they weren't ever. Fuck, Ray. You're sounding crazy now! A fucking girl you never even fucked dumps you poorly and you're freaking out! It happens! Sometimes girls are bitches, and sometimes they even have good reasons to be! We don't know! We just know that she's gone. And if she wanted to talk to you, she would have."

"What if that was her that came to the Hole a month ago?"

"Yeah, what if I could shoot lasers out of my dick? Boy, that would be great! Ray, fuck, man. Don't hold on to this. Move on. You've got other friends, you've got other girls."

Ray thought. Ogami was right. His life wasn't as bad as he made it out to be. He had friends and that was important. His friends were the high point of his life at this stage. Which made being abandoned by one all the more unacceptable. But maybe that is the way it went down. Shit happens, Ray knew this. He'd seen more than his share of fucked up behavior from all sorts of folks.

But not from Jenny.

"She didn't dump me. She's my friend and I stand by my friends. And so would she."

Ogami sighed again. "She was cool as fuck. But she's gone. Deal with it and don't let this fuck you up. Besides, what are you going to do? Tell the cops that this friend you haven't seen in a few months might be in trouble but you don't know why or where or in what way? That you've got a bad feeling because you don't think she'd fuck you over like this?"

When put like that, Ray knew it was a stupid idea. He had probably run Jenny off at some point. Or she had just found something better or more interesting. Or she got married. There were a lot of explanations and Ray would have to live without knowing which, if any, were right. He was a private detective, but this wasn't his kind of "case." This wasn't a mystery to solve. It was just a shitty thing that happened in a world full of shitty things and awesome things.

"I wonder what that symbol is, though. Did she design it? Maybe she's big time now because of it. She blew us off for, uh, I dunno, symbol designing?"

"You said that hot girl you saw naked had that as a tattoo, right?"

"Yeah," Ray said. "Next time I shoot her, I'll ask. That wouldn't be too creepy, would it? She told me not to be creepy."

"Dude, a lot of people get tattoos just so that people will say, 'Hey that's awesome! What is it?' Remember Todd?"

Ray started laughing immediately. Todd had been a friend of theirs for some reason, even though no one in the group was sure whose friend he was originally. He was an all right guy, but he was really proud of his tattoos. He'd expose them at any opportunity, just waiting for someone to take the bait and talk about them. Once he'd hooked someone, they weren't going to be open for conversation with anyone else for at least a couple hours. It had been a running joke until he moved back to Wisconsin.

"Ah, fuck," Ray said. "Heh. So, uh, what you up to tonight?"

"Date with Soph. She was DD last night so I got to treat her well. Nice food, no t-shirts, the whole deal. Sorry, man."

"No, no worries. Sounds fun," Ray really didn't feel jealous of Soph. She was a great girl who deserved special treatment. He was always glad when his friend was making sure to treat her right. "I should probably take the night off, anyway. Develop those photos."

"Yeah! Get to see that girl again, the hot one, right? You should develop extra copies of some of hers and keep them! It's like your own private porno stash! Except, even more private!"

"Oh, God. I'm not that desperate, am I?" Ray asked.

"Dude, you were convinced there was a conspiracy to remove Jenny from your life just a minute ago."

"Good point. So tonight is me, my 'photo lab' and some alone time."

"Remember to wash your hands before jerking off. Don't want to get all those chemicals in your dickhole."

"Ah, Jesus!" Ray screamed. "Fuck! Bad ball tingle!"

"Ahhh, the burning, the burning!"

"SHUT UP, O!" But Ray couldn't help but laugh. "Shit. Tonight should be kind of fun, actually. Do some work. I think some of the photos will turn out actually good. I'll order some Chinese—"

"Food or hookers?"

"What's the difference? You get really excited about both, but feel really gross and unsatisfied afterwards."

# CHAPTER SIXTEEN

Back at his apartment, Ray sat down and lit a cigarette. He took the time to sit and enjoy it. He had no pressing concerns. He put a mixtape Jenny'd made him on and decided just to appreciate what they'd shared already. He looked at the rolls of film in their little plastic coffins. Or wombs, more. Uteri? They weren't quite born yet. It was a lot of photos, so Ray knew he had better get started. He turned the music up so he could hear it in his bathroom and went to work.

He was used to working in the dark at this point. He remembered when he had first started. He had fucked up roll after roll after roll of film. The whole transfer process of opening the plastic holder, breaking in, and retrieving the film had seemed nigh-unto-impossible. His first photography class had nicknamed him "Yosemite Sam" due to his tendency to let out a string of angry expletives every time he screwed up.

It was Jenny, actually, that had helped him get a system down for doing it. Ray smiled as he effortlessly cracked open one roll and began the chemical treatments. He decided to do all of the rolls before checking any of them.

Later, holding the negatives up to the light, he saw a lot of good possibilities. Unsurprisingly, most of the ones that looked really good featured Cassandra. Ray began to wonder how exactly he could ask her out, or if he could at all. She seemed a bit out of his league. And was paid to have sex with other men.

But he wasn't thinking of marriage. Ogami was right, it had been too long since Ray had dated. He used to be able to do so fairly well. He was never a Don Juan like Ogami, but he'd done OK for himself. Maybe having a female best friend HAD hurt him, after all. Girls may have seen her as too much of a threat, or something.

As he started developing the shots, he felt pretty good about most of them. The lighting was shit, of course, but he had done everything he could to make up for it. A few were almost gallery-worthy. He'd certainly have put them in his portfolio, back when anyone looked at it. Frankie should be happy. This was going to be the finest-shot semi-amateur porno around.

Ray wondered if this would lead to more photography work. He had heard that the Playboy photogs were paid pretty well, as far as freelancers go. Maybe from there, he could branch out to all those stupid "men's magazines" with inane articles and stupid cheesecake photos. Not what he'd dreamed of in art school, but better than fat people's private lives by a long shot.

He stopped and looked at a nice shot of Cassandra sucking Steven's dick. Her tattoo was plainly visible there. That would be his "in." He's ask about the tattoo, sound cool for seeing it and noticing it, and from there it would be easy sailing.

Ray laughed at himself, knowing that flirting hadn't been "easy sailing" for him in years, if it ever had been at all. But something seemed easier, at least.


He finished with the photos and hung them to dry throughout the bathroom. He went into his other room and called up the local Chinese joint, run, of course, by Mexicans. The Mexican place down the street? Run by Chinese folks. If it were expensive or in a different part of Vegas, this would be called "fusion." As it was, it was only "shitty."

As he waited, he continued to listen to the music, and actually picked up his place a bit. Clearly, he didn't have places to put everything that was lying around, but he found that even putting them in pseudo-stacks seemed to improve the general feeling of the apartment. Soon he found that he could walk around barefoot and not step on anything that hurt.

A Mexican man on a bicycle soon delivered his "Chinese" food: chicken wings and steamed dumplings. They were almost enjoyable. He ate too fast and got stomach cramps again. Nothing like MexiChinese food to bring them back.

After some unpleasantly productive time in the bathroom, Ray sat on his futon and thought about what to do next. Ogami and Soph were out. He had planned on staying in all night, but every time he did this, he seemed to forget what exactly that entailed.

When Ray had money, he had plenty of things to do. TV, books, nights out, the sky was the limit. Well, somewhere between the sky and the dirt, actually. But Ray no longer had a TV (he only missed it on nights like these), nor much of a stereo(let alone anything that played music without you putting some kind of disk or tape in it), nor did he buy new books anymore (as he found the expense was rarely worth the risk anymore; it's easy to read when you're comfortable).

He had eaten. He had done his photography work. He had cleaned all he cared to clean for the night. And now Ray found himself itching like hell for something to do. Ogami and Soph were still out of the question. Ray no longer had a long list of friends to call. He looked at his phone's list of numbers. There was Ogami, Soph, Frankie, Amy, and Jenny.

Jenny. It was OK not to call Jenny anymore. She'd turned her back on him. She left without telling anyone. Ray was perfectly fine now. Except for the sweat on his hands. Ray stood up and started walking back and forth in his apartment, a nervous energy building within him with no release in sight.

Ray wasn't worried about why she left. Ray wasn't worried that he'd done something stupid some drunken night that he didn't even remember. Ray wasn't worried that something awful had happened to her, and he wasn't around to help. Ray wasn't worried at all. No sir.

"Goddammit," he said and walked outside. Ray knew that he was just not used to having so little to do. He hated being cooped up for this long a period, even though he never could remember this fact. He walked out of the apartment and just kept on walking. He had walked for half an hour before realizing he had no destination in mind.

He took out his phone and called Amy. His only other choice was Frankie at this point. It rang. *'Fuck, I'm calling a seventeen year old girl on a Saturday night. I'm a fucking pederast! Jesus Christ!'* It rang again. *'Fuck, I really have to hang up. This is stupid. But I'm so goddam bored. Shit, she probably doesn't want to talk to me anyway. Probably out with someone cool and her own age. Or cooler and older than me. Whatever. Fuck.'*

"Hello. You've reached Amy Gordon. Please leave your name and number at the beep. Have a nice day!"

"Uhhhh, it's, uh, it's Ray. Um, yeah. Bye." Ray hung up with even more disgust than his usual post-message-leaving feeling. *'Oh, well. She won't call back now, so it's out of my hands.'*

Having no other reasonable person to call, Ray decided to just head to the Hole and see what turned up there. It was still fairly early, so he decided to walk. This was a decision he came to regret about halfway there and four cigarettes through.

By the time he actually got there, he was exhausted, hungry, and holding in a mighty hot burst of diarrhea. He ran straight to the bathroom and his body didn't even wait until he sat down. There was an ichorous dark brown spray on the back of the toilet and dripping down his leg. "Goddammit!" he screamed. He then remembered he didn't want any company, so he decided to curse quietly from that point on. He quickly pulled out a huge wad of toilet paper and mopped up his leg. "Fuck." It took a few tries to really get it somewhere close to maybe being comfortable.

He then looked at the mess he made on and around the toilet. "Aw, goddammit," he sighed. It was a bar, though, and a dive at that. He loved this dive, but it was still a dive. It had no doubt seen worse than this fecal gift in its time. Ray desperately searched for a way not to feel bad about not cleaning it up himself. It occurred to him that bourbon might be his best bet.

He walked out of the bathroom and slowly up to the bar, failing to be inconspicuous as only someone who could still tell there used to be shit on his leg can. He looked around for familiar faces. He saw a few folks that he recognized and didn't know.

He and Jenny had often nicknamed some of the "recurring extras" in their lives, the people they saw often but never really knew. There was "the Explorer," who always wore a backpack and seemed to constantly be reaching new territory with wide eyes. There was "Dungeon Master," the chubby fellow with the terrible beard and the pony-tail that took classes with them from time to time. Ray recognized the man he knew only as "Chinese Groucho" at a corner seat, but that was as close as he got to knowing anyone.

Martin, a tall black man, was tending the bar. Ray didn't know him too well. "Hey, Martin," he said, sitting down. Martin gave a nod. "Uh, I was just, uh, in the bathroom," Ray heard himself begin, "and, uh, I think someone made a mess in there. It was, uh, pretty gross." Deflection worked sometimes. Ray wondered why he felt the need to deflect before anyone even said anything.

"Yeah, someone, huh?" was Martin's only reply.

"Yeah," Ray stuck to his lies whenever possible.

"Hey, Paolo!" Martin called to a heavily tattooed Mexican cleaner back in the kitchen. "**Some**body made a big goddam mess in the men's bathroom! Can you clean that up?"

Before Ray could look away, Paolo shot him a rather angry look. Ray tried to look confused and innocent, but that didn't change the look.

"You gonna order something?" Martin asked. "Or is your stomach too fucked up?"

"No, uh, I'm fine. I'll have a bourbon." Ray remembered he had some spending money. "Woodford Reserve, please. Straight, three fingers."

"Bourbon, huh? No wonder you're running to the bathroom."

"Uhm," Ray said dumbly.

"Don't sweat it, man. I'm just fuckin' with you. Paolo's a real asshole motherfucker. You can do whatever you want in there and I'll thank you for it."

"Uh, OK," Ray replied, still not sure where he stood.

"Aren't you Ogami's friend?" Martin asked. Ray nodded. "I thought I recognized you. How is that motherfucker?"

"Good," Ray said. "Out with his girlfriend tonight."

"Goddam. He's one lucky son of a bitch, right? Girl like that? Shit, only comes once in a lifetime."

"Yeah," Ray agreed. "Soph is great. She's really cool, too."

"A fucking trapeze girl? From fucking Brazil? Shit, you gotta be kidding me. Lucky motherfucker . . ."

Ray let him trail off, unsure himself as to what to say at that point.

"Hey," Martin said at last. "Speaking of fine ladies, you still with that white girl with the laugh?"

There was no doubt as to the subject of Martin's question. Of all her endearing qualities, one that stuck out most immediately to casual observers was Jenny's laugh. It somehow achieved the perfect harmony between infectious, cute, and raucous. It was a hallmark of her simultaneously girlish and boyish appeal that left people of all genders and orientations confused.

"Uh, no. Well, really, we weren't ever dating. She was my friend."

"Friends like that, who needs dating?" Martin laughed. "Hey, could you introduce me?"

"No!" Ray realized too late how forcefully he said it. "I mean, I don't really see her that much anymore. For a few months. Uh, I think she moved or something."

"Oh," Martin said quietly. "Uh, that sucks." Once again, Ray had succeeded in making someone else feel as awkward as he did.

"Yeah," he agreed. He took a deep swig of the bourbon and felt it hit his stomach. He had shat out everything he'd eaten, and the long walk had made him hungry. "Uh, could I get a burger?" he asked.

"Yeah, no problem. I just won't tell Paolo."

Ray smiled and continued his drinking. He lit a cigarette and took in a deep, satisfying toke. He had stopped at a gas station along the way and bought some respectable Camels. The taste was surprisingly pleasing to him after years of cheap knock-offs. He had forgotten just what a good cigarette was like.

Martin soon returned with a greasy burger and fries. The burgers at the Hole in the Wall Bar weren't masterpieces, or really anywhere close. They were, in fact, rather average. But there was some kind of appeal there that Ray could not place. There was something about bar burgers in general. It's like the meat somehow soaked up all the smoke and the fumes from the booze and became altogether different from any other kind of meat. A bar burger was never great, but it always hit the spot.

Ray loved bars. When he was young, his parents took him to their local pub for dinner occasionally. Ray had explained this to some friends, who immediately assumed his parents were career alcoholics. People who didn't love bars were never able to understand the appeal. The air stank, the people were largely sad losers, and they were by and large either seedy or snobby. But the seediness was a home, a comfort to other people. Ray felt a sense of tranquility and rightness when at a bar. He could look around and see other people, some sad, some happy. It was a constant reminder that the world outside of Ray moved on. The world moved on. Sad people became happy. Happy people became sad.

## CHAPTER SEVENTEEN

The danger of going to a bar by himself was that Ray often waxed oddly philosophical about the most mundane of things. Bars themselves, for instance. Ray shook his head at himself and ordered another bourbon. A couple bourbons later he found himself doodling the a/star symbol on a napkin. He wanted to talk to Cassandra.

To contact her, he had to contact Frankie. This seemed distasteful at first, but Ray thought about how well Frankie had always treated him. Jobs, money, the offers of women. Frankie was a sleaze ball, of this there was no doubt. But maybe he was an OK guy, too. He knew this was most likely the drink talking, but he had already dialed the number and stepped outside.

"Hello, who's calling?" Ray heard Frankie answer.

"It's Ray."

"Ray Brautigan, my boy! How are you doing, huh?"

"I'm OK, Frankie. How are you?"

"Hey, I'm Frankie! You know I am always good! But Ray, you are not a phone call man. You do not call me for small talk, and I respect that. Why is it you call me now?"

Ray found it more difficult than he planned to get out what he wanted. "Um, uh, at the, uh, shoot the other night?"

"Yes, the shoot," Frankie prodded gently.

"Um, that girl, Cassandra?"

"Oh, yes, beautiful girl. I knew you would like her. I picked her for you, you know that? I thought, Ray, he is a man of high taste in ladies. He will like Cassandra."

"Uh, yeah. I, uh, do."

"Yes, I saw you talking to her all the night! I even tried to get you fucking her! But you two, you were shy, I could tell."

"Right," Ray felt all the world like he was in study hall passing notes. This was so stupid. "I was wondering if, uh, we were doing any more work with her soon."

"Oh, Ray my boy! You want to see Cassandra! Why do you not just go ahead and ask me? She does not whore, I do not think, but maybe I could —"

"No, no, no. I don't want to hire her or anything. Uh, I, I just wanted to know how to get in touch with her, uh, if I could."

"Oh, you are a gentleman, I should have known! Ray, my boy, Ray Brautigan, please take no offense if I have made some. I only want to treat my boy right, and I am never sure how to do this!"

"Uh, it's OK, Frankie. I'm not offended or anything. But do you know how to, uh, contact her?" Ray was actually shaking in the warm Nevada air. It was nonsense.

"I tell you what, I look around, I find out, I call you back. OK? I call you back on this phone, Ray, my boy. Ah, beautiful Cassandra and handsome fuck man Ray! I knew it in my heart! I will call you back!"

But Ray was less sure what he was getting into. He hadn't bothered dating in a long time. Was Cassandra really the place to start? She was beautiful, yes. And smart, and cool, and fun. And it shouldn't matter that she danced or did porn. In theory, that should make her hotter.

But it made Ray feel a bit dirty. It was a little close to prostitution, a subject which made him feel extremely guilty. He'd succumbed to its attraction during a few drunken nights and experienced a shame spiral for weeks afterward every time. The very tenuous connection was already making him nervous. What if she was dirty?

Ray was immediately furious with himself for thinking this. He felt racist and sexist and generally like an old conservative asshole. He should be enlightened and feel great about whatever Cassandra chose to do for a living. But what if she WAS dirty? As much as he wanted contact with a woman, he wanted to keep a sore-free dick even more.

Back inside and nursing another bourbon, he saw how stupid he was being. Even if Frankie found a way to contact her, she'd most likely want nothing to do with him. He was the least creepy of a group of extremely creepy people that she met at a place that she'd probably not want to be reminded of. And she was beautiful. She most likely had some hot, muscular boyfriend. He was a skinny white nerd, a curiosity like an anteater in her life. Something interesting to talk to once or twice, but not date material. She'd have no interest in him.

Hell, Jenny sure didn't. She was his best friend and she up and left without so much as a goodbye. He'd probably creeped her out, too. He remembered telling her he loved her once, just a bit before never seeing her again. He had done his best to explain that he loved her like he loved Ogami, and she had seemed to understand and even return the affection. But that's not the sort of thing girls hear and take lightly. He had scared her off, probably, and they'd never dance to Elvis singing gospel music again.

Ray drained the bourbon and cursed himself. He knew he was waiting for phone calls. He seemed to do that a lot these days. Waiting for Jenny to call. Waiting for Frankie to call. To call back, both of them. He wasn't totally inactive, some passive anti-hero. He tried, he really did. But they just weren't calling back. Amy wasn't calling back.

This relieved Ray. He was totally lost about what to do with her. Every time he thought about her he felt good and then he felt horny and then he felt guilty. In high school, he'd hated it when girls his age dated older guys, even by a couple of years. He wondered what kind of losers they were that they couldn't get dates their own age. And now his best female friend was almost half his age and he was ashamed to want to fuck her.

New bourbon in hand, he tried not to think about how much he wanted to fuck Amy. God, she was so soft. And that apple smell, that reminder that she was a woman. Her breasts were bigger than those on most girls he had dated, and they excited him.

"Fuck," Ray said to no one. He had let his mind wander where it didn't need to go. Amy was too young. It was stupid and he was old and he was disgusting and that was it. He wondered if that is why he found Cassandra attractive. At least she was around his age. And he wouldn't feel disgusting next to her, at least until they got naked. "Who am I kidding?" he said aloud again.

He was drunk now, at a bar, alone. Waiting for phone calls that would not be coming. He felt stupid. "Goddammit," he said and he put down a sizable tip and left the bar. "Fuck," he repeated, again to no one. He walked.

He later found himself pissing in an alley. A cat meowed at him. He told it to fuck off. It did. He walked more. He saw some garbage men. He helped them put garbage in their truck. They laughed and he said "OK, it's OK." He walked more. At some point he may have seen that symbol again on someone's car. Or a wall. He couldn't be sure.

By the time he got home, his head had cleared a bit, but not his mood. He was pissing in his toilet when he saw a picture of Cassandra that he liked. He took it to his futon and started to masturbate. Pangs of creepy guilt hindered his arousal and he eventually fell asleep with his dick out.

This was embarrassing but at least made pissing the next morning one step easier. He thought about trying again but decided against it. He picked up his phone to charge it and was surprised to see he actually missed a call. Frankie, probably. Jenny's not calling, that's for sure.

He dialed his voicemail and listened. "Hey, Ray Brautigan, my boy! It is me, your pal Frankie. It took me a while, but I have a way to contact the beautiful girl for you." Ray freaked out, trying to find a pen to write down the information. He had to replay the message twice to actually get it down. After that, he listened and heard he still had a message. He knew he must have slept heavily to miss two phone calls.

"Hey, Ray, it's Amy. Nice message, dweeb! It really cracked me up. So, yeah, it's late and it's Saturday but give me a call. Bye!"

Ray officially was bewildered. He now had the option to call two attractive girls. Either the past few years were about to karmically be repaid, or something very goddam strange was going on. At this point, Ray cared not. He cared only for breakfast. He craved eggs, but hesitated. Eggs would mean a diner. That would also mean bacon. This, on top of the previous day's digestive mishaps was not such a swift idea. Ray knew this.

But once he had thought of bacon, he knew there was no stopping until the lust for pig fat was sated. Ray needed the Greasy Spoon.

The Greasy Spoon was perhaps generically named. But it was aptly named. It was a quintessential diner. The waitresses were sassy and uniformed. Their accent seemed to be freshly imported from Brooklyn. And everything was full of grease. Delicious, wonderful grease. Ray caught an early bus and was there within fifteen minutes.

Ray was a regular in several bars throughout town. He would be recognized by quite a few bartenders. But Ray had always wanted to be a regular at the Greasy Spoon. He wanted one of those large, loud women to remember what he always ordered and to chat with him about inane things.

He would, if this happened, of course lie. Nothing about his life seemed suitable to talk about with senior citizens, even diner waitresses. He and Jenny had planned several possible alternate lives to the last detail. Names were rehearsed, occupations selected, and histories mapped out.

It was all for naught, as Ray had, in all his years of patronage, never been recognized. He was afraid that he seemed to be one of the ironic hipsters that frequented the joint. The waitresses clearly preferred the actual blue collar working men and women to the artsy types enjoying their stupid kitsch. And Ray kind of *was* an artsy type, but he liked to think that he wasn't like the hipsters. Certainly, they'd never want to actually hang out with him.

"Hey, honey," one of them said to him. "Whattaya want?"

"Salami, egg, and bacon sandwich. Um, uh, small tomato juice and, uh, large, uh, orange juice," Ray said, undue hope in his hesitant voice. The waitress' name was Tammy, according to her name tag. Her uniform was light blue and kept fairly well for its obvious age. She nodded her grey head.

"Get that right to ya," she said and she meant it. Ray looked around at the other customers. Mexican laborers ready to do some work on Sunday, hipsters coming down from the previous night's ironic festivities, and old men on the way to some worship service. Ray knew where his loyalties were.

Even at the height of his success, Ray had mixed feelings about art. He "knew" photography was what he was best at, that he wanted to make art. But he always felt more than a little guilty. He was not so sure that art was the most productive use of anyone's time or money. There was something Ray preferred in the proverbial "honest day's labor." Ray harbored a weird kind of envy for people whose jobs seemed to actually affect the world in more than an aesthetical manner.

Now he was neither here nor there. He wasn't an artist by any means, nor an honest worker with a "real job." He was the sort of scum that could only exist in a shitty city like Las Vegas. He was a parasite in the intestinal tract of society.

With that appetizing thought, Ray's breakfast arrived. It was exactly what he wanted. The salami was fresh, the eggs perfectly fried, and the bacon crisp and full of delicious pork fat. The sandwich filled his mouth with a savory beauty, the taste of morning in America. The orange juice was freshly squeezed and filled with tasty pulp. And the tomato juice finished off the meal perfectly.

There was something to be said for actually eating food in the morning that didn't come in a packet. After Ray left the diner, he felt an energy he lacked most any other morning. Properly fueled, his body actually felt like lasting the entire day. And his stomach was giving no protest, for once. He lit a fresh cigarette and inhaled deeply. It gave the sharp satisfaction of an after-meal smoke and the slight buzz that often came with it.

He was going to call Cassandra today. It felt right, it felt time. She was pretty, she showed him kindness. This was more than he'd received from other women of late, except for Amy. And Amy, he reminded himself again, would probably be a huge mistake. The stripper had less trouble potential than the teenager, despite what American media might say on the subject.

# CHAPTER EIGHTEEN

Ray got back on the bus and the warmth coming in the windows made Ray actually feel rather cozy. His eyes drooped a bit and his head began to fall as well. On one trip down his eyes vaguely registered a familiar shape. That blue shirt . . .Jenny had had one like it.

Ray's head shot back up and he craned his neck to see if it was her. He couldn't see and scratched around for the button to signal he wanted to get off. He found it, still looking for any sign of the blue shirt. He pressed it and the bus drove on for three more blocks before reaching a stop. Ray knew it was most likely too late, but he got off anyway, even after a moment's hesitation. He started walking back to where he thought he saw the shirt and realized the foolishness of the endeavor. While falling asleep he thought he saw a shirt that looked like one of Jenny's shirts. What was he doing?

She had left. She had left and probably because of him. She left to get away from Ray. And here he was still searching for her, heart still going erratic at the sight of a shirt that may have been hers. Ray cursed himself and darkly walked back to the bus stop.

He no longer felt excitement about calling Cassandra. He felt only dread. Another girl with no reason to find him interesting. Another girl that might befriend him for a while and leave. Another reason to feel shitty and to drink alone.

But Jenny wasn't a date, she was a friend. Ray reminded himself that he wasn't dumped by a girlfriend, he was abandoned by a good friend. Ogami was full of shit. Jenny was a great friend, but she was nothing more. It would feel this way no matter what friend up and left. It's just that no other friend would do this.

And he never thought Jenny would either.

The bus arrived and Ray got on it. The heat no longer felt soothing, it was oppressive. The womb-like coziness was completely gone. It was just him and a lot of feeling bad this time.

His phone rang and he almost decided to ignore it. But the only thing worse than being miserable was being miserable and alone, so he answered. "Ray Brautigan."

"Ray Brautigan, my boy! It is Frankie, your old friend!"

"Oh. Hi." Ray no longer saw Frankie as a warm, silly old man. He was back to being a creepy son of a bitch Ray was embarrassed to need. Once again, a single thought of Jenny had reversed his entire mood.

"So, did you call the beautiful babe Cassandra? I left you a message with her phone number."

"Oh, uh, no, I didn't call."

"Ah, you are waiting, eh? It is too early for beautiful woman. You call now, you seem desperate, like you never get hot fuck dates. My boy Ray Brautigan is very clever."

"Um, yeah, I dunno." Back when he was going to call her, he WAS going to call her way too early. Frankie apparently had better skills with women than he did. This epiphany did not improve Ray's mood.

"So, you have the pictures for me? I will be at Melanie's watching the pussies and the titties dancing. Come bring them."

"Uh, when? I'm not home right now."

"You come soon. Come to Melanie's, I will be there as usual. We have good possibilities with these photographs of hot video store fuck action."

"Right," Ray said. "I'll be there. Nothing else to do. Bye." Ray hung up before Frankie could prattle on any further. Maybe he'd bring some extra cash and actually spend time with some dancers. Never have to worry about how they felt. They hated him and made no bones about it. Their honesty was refreshing in this day and age.

At home, Ray gathered the photos and put them in his briefcase in a portfolio. They were still good photos, but now the pictures of Cassandra didn't arouse him; they just made him feel worse. And the ones with her and Steven made him feel sick. He shoved them away and left quickly, ready to be rid of the entire bunch.

He made his way to Melanie's at a sickening early hour for such a trip. Other cities had strip clubs. Other cities no doubt had depressing, creepy strip clubs like Melanie's. But other cities had the good sense to keep them closed until ungodly hours where sin was more welcome. Las Vegas kept their titty shacks open twenty four hours a day, because there was always some local pervert or slumming tourist ready to see for pay what he could get for free after a couple beers.

The crowd on the bus was even worse than the last time he'd made this journey. The type of person going to a red light area before sundown is not the type that anyone would want to associate themselves with. It made him want another shower. He was going to have to wait a while.

Melanie's was even uglier by day. The outside was last painted sometime in the late seventies. The sign was missing letters and in an outdated font. It was strangely free of graffiti, but maybe the taggers just thought the place would be an embarrassment to their reputation.

The bouncer nodded at Ray. Couldn't be a regular at the Greasy Spoon, but he sure was here. Wonderful. Ray walked in and saw that a couple of girls he hadn't seen before were dancing. There were only two men there other than Frankie, neither paid him any mind.

There was Frankie, getting a lap dance from another new girl. She . . .wasn't completely disgusting. Frankie had buried his face in her bare breasts far enough that he didn't see Ray come in. Ray looked around and had nowhere else to sit as far as he could figure, so he sat in Frankie's corner, wondering where to look.

"Oh, Ray my boy, I did not see you!" Frankie said as the girl had gotten on her knees in front of him to rub her hair on Frankie's crotch, or where it would be if his fat gut hadn't drifted over it. "I was distracted by Matisha's large dark titties in my face! You want a dance?"

Ray shook his head. "I brought the pictures."

"Yes, yes. Business Ray Brautigan, you make me laugh with your seriousness. Matisha, we will finish our encounter at another time. My boy Ray Brautigan wants to do business."

"Whateva," she drawled. "I do what I want." She left them to a back room.

Ray took his case out and gave Frankie the portfolio. "Here," he said, looking around. Some other girls walked around, looking for suckers willing to drop a twenty on a lap dance. Frankie opened the portfolio and began looking through the pictures.

"Ohhh. Ray, this is number one top notch! These make my boner bigger than Matisha's black titties did! Oh, Ray, this is best I have had. Ray, we will make tall piles of cash money for this! We should do this again and again, become like the big boys of hot fuck action here!"

Ray had never seen Frankie so excited. It was not pleasant. "Yeah, OK, whatever," he said.

"The money will be more and more. We will become rich motherfuckers and even I will get all the hot pussy I want, just like you! You going to fuck beautiful Cassandra tonight?"

Ray just shook his head.

"But why not? I get you the number! That was not easy even for me!"

For a moment, Ray almost explained why. But, trying to articulate it, he didn't really know. Anyway, his personal business should be kept far away from Frankie at all costs. Frankie didn't need to know shit of shit about his life, Jenny, or anything else.

"I dunno. Bad mood, I guess," he felt was a vague enough explanation to get Frankie off his ass without giving him any details.

"Bad mood, Ray Brautigan? You need fuck action. Goddammit, Ray. You call that Cassandra or I send nastiest hooker I know to your apartment with gun to fuck you or kill you."

Ray stared at him.

Frankie broke out into a smile. "I kid. I kid about the killing. Not about the fuck action. You need it. I see it in your eyes. You need it, Ray. You at least need night out with something soft. Ray, even when you do not fuck them, a woman can change your mood."

Ray was a little alarmed that Frankie was apparently thinking more clearly than he was. "Yeah, maybe I will," he said. "See you later, Frankie."

"Of course, my boy. We will take more pictures soon. Maybe with a new girlfriend Cassandra! And you be the star. I kid, I kid."

Ray smiled and left. Frankie was right. There was no reason not to at least call Cassandra. Worst thing that would happen was a disgusted "No," and that would leave him no different than he was already.  He headed home, readying himself for the inevitable call.

.

# CHAPTER NINETEEN

Once home again, he looked at his bourbon jug. His impulse was to down a big swig to calm his nerves. On the ride home they'd started to make him more and more jittery. Nothing like a cold call to a beautiful woman to fuck with someone's head.

He poured himself a drink and stared at the glass. "Ah, fuck it," he said aloud and grabbed his phone anyway. He dialed the numbers and felt dizzy.

One ring.

Two rings.

Three rings. *'She's not answering,'* he thought. *'Maybe she sees my name on her phone. Oh, God. She's not answering. A message. I hate messages.'*

"Hello," someone answered. "Hello?"

"Uhhhh, Cassandra?" Ray spat out, mouth dry as cotton.

"Speaking. Who is this? Stan?"

*'Who the fuck is Stan? Oh, shit, probably her boyfriend,'* Ray thought. "Uh, it's Ray. Ray Brautigan."

There was a pause. "Who?" A thousand curses ran through Ray's head at once. This was going even more poorly than he'd feared.

"Uh, Ray. I, uh, we, um, we met the other night." How to put this? "Uh, at the . . . at the video store."

"At the video store? I . . . oh! Oh! Ray! The photographer!"

"Uh, yeah. That's me." The silence between sentences was like a gut shot from a twelve gauge.

"Uh, hi. Um . . . no offense, but how'd you get this number?"

"Uhhhhh . . .Frankie, uh, I asked Frankie for it." Ray wanted to hang up immediately.

"Oh. Um, how are you?"

"Uh, good. Good. How are, uh, you?" Small talk was no less painful.

"I'm, uh, fine. Um, what's up? Is there another job or something?"

"Huh? Oh, uh, no. I, uh, I just wanted to call you. Uh, myself." At this point he froze again. "Um, I wanted to, uh, see you. Uh."

The pause was even longer this time. "Uh, I don't do, uh, that kind of job. Uh," she said, as awkwardly as Ray.

"Huh? Oh, God, no. No, not a job at all. I wanted, to, uh . . .ask you . . .uh, out."

"Ask me out? Like on a date?"

At this point there was no going back at all. "Yes. Yes I am."

"Are you being creepy?" she asked. Ray wanted to rip his ears off. "I'm just kidding! Wow. I can't remember the last time someone actually called me up to ask me out."

"Oh. Uh, do people not, uh, do that these days?"

"I think they do. I dunno. Just, uh, not to me. You know, you just kind of meet people and hang out or whatever."

"Uh, yeah, I guess," Ray wasn't getting an answer.

"Um, so. Asking me out. Uh, yeah. Yeah! We can go out. When?" She said yes. She said yes. What now?

"Um, I'm free, uh, a lot."

"That's encouraging," she said. "What about, well, what about tonight? I'm off tomorrow anyway."

"Uh, yeah. I'm free. Definitely. So, do we, uh, go see a movie or something?"

"I dunno. I don't think so. Nothing good out. How about, you know, like, dinner and drinks or something?"

"Yeah. Yeah! Yeah, dinner. That would be fun. Um, I . . ."

"Do you like sushi?" she asked.

"Yeah, I do. I do. Sushi's good." Ray was babbling.

"OK. I know a place. You don't have a car, right?"

"Right," Ray said with embarrassment.

"Hey, me neither. Want to meet at the place?" Ray agreed. "OK, it's called Oikawa Sushi. It's on Sahara near Arville."

"Uh, yeah, OK. Like, when?" Ray was bad at making plans, so he was happy Cassandra didn't seem to be.

"Six OK for you?" she asked.

"Yeah, it's great. So, yeah, Oikawa Sushi at six. Yeah. You remember what I look like? I'll wear, uh, I'll wear a blue shirt and a tie."

"No tie, just the shirt," she said. "I remember you. Nerdy with glasses." She laughed a bit. Ray's heart sank a bit, too. "With nice lips." It rose quite a bit more. "You remember me?"

"Definitely," he said, a bit too fast.

"I guess so, if you're willing to call Frankie just to get my number. OK, I gotta go get ready. See you then!"

"Bye," Ray said and hung up. He immediately began to freak the fuck out. He jumped up and danced a little bit. In celebration, he downed the glass of bourbon he'd poured before making the call. He whooped and hollered like a college football fan on serious amphetamines. A date, a real date, with a really hot girl.

Ray didn't have much getting ready to do. He boiled up a hot dog for lunch, and took out his nicest blue shirt. He went to the mirror and looked at himself. He needed another shave if he was going to have a date. Except some girls like the scruffy look. He looked at his lips. They were nice? He'd never thought of his lips. He always thought that if he had an attractive feature (he rarely thought he did), then it was his hair. But maybe girls don't really give a shit about that.

Ray began to wonder about what might happen. Sushi dinner, that was pretty cool. It sounded like the kind of place that actually makes their own sushi, rare in this town.

What if they fucked? Ray tried to push the question out of his head, but there was no denying he wanted it. And he'd seen that she does, in fact have sex. But maybe that was just professional? He knew he shouldn't expect anything. But the thought lingered, and, just in case, he went to his futon and masturbated. The last thing he wanted, was IF they ended up fucking, spurting in the first ten seconds. This might buy him a few more minutes. If they fucked. Big if.

He didn't need to pull out any porn this time. His mind was filled with thoughts of Cassandra. He'd seen enough of her to make this easy. He began stroking and his mind wandered through various fantasies. She blew him at the sushi place, fucked him in the bathroom, fucked him in his apartment, and, oddly, fucked him in the film developing room at UNLV.

Inevitably, he also thought of other women. A hot girl from high school begging for his cock. Angelina Jolie throwing him to the floor. Taking Amy from behind.

He stopped for a moment and refocused his mind on Cassandra. Beating off to Amy was inappropriate, he told himself, and concentrated on an elaborate scenario with Cassandra in a nurse's outfit and soon came hard.

It was the best jerking off session he'd had in recent memory. He was left sweaty and sleepy. "Jesus," he said. He went to his bathroom and cleaned himself off. He corked the bourbon, scared he'd do something stupid if he got drunk first.

Early as he was, Ray couldn't stand the tedium anymore so he grabbed a wad of cash and headed out. Flowers. Flowers would be nice. Or they'd be dorky. Ray really couldn't tell. She had teased him about being nerdy already, so maybe she was one of those fabled nerd-chasers. He'd always heard that some girls were into that kind of guy for whatever reason. He's just not ever benefited from it personally. This could be his chance. He went to a local florist.

It was filled with chintzy flowers, mostly artificial. He found some real ones that looked pretty, some kind of blue flower, and paid for them. He was beginning to feel good about the whole thing. *'And to think, I owe it all to Frankie. Jesus Christ.'*

He couldn't help but smile. His mind wandered to years down the road, a wedding in a nice chapel, Ogami as the best man, and Frankie the guest of honor. That's probably the only time "honor" would ever be used in conjunction with Frankie's name.

He walked by bar after bar. It was best to stay completely in control for this. He had enough of a tendency to say stupid shit that ran women off when sober, boozing before she started boozing was out of the question. He walked over to Sahara and waited for the bus.

It came and he noticed the passengers. Not the filth he was used to dealing with. These are people that, if you had children, you wouldn't hide the kids' eyes when they were around. It wasn't the king of England, but at least they showed signs of proper human grooming.

He sat and watched his surroundings improve as he got further from his neighborhood. The men wore shirts, and the women wore clothes that fit. The children didn't run into the street at random times and the animals were actually pets, not strays. It was still mostly strip malls, but there were fewer and fewer obvious "body work" joints and more and more places where people could actually buy products. Whether or not they actually needed them was up for plenty of debate, but at least it was legal.

The Washington stop arrived far earlier than he'd thought it would. Ray could never estimate time or distances, and when he had to estimate the time to go a distance, he was doubly fucked. It was a full hour before he was supposed to meet Cassandra and there he was. Huckleberry's across the way seemed to be a decent enough bar, but Ray reminded himself that wasn't the best idea.

He had a sudden panic attack. What was he going to talk about with Cassandra? Didn't seem like a great idea to talk about how they met. He didn't want to just go on and on about his own life, especially considering how it had fallen into a toilet at some point in the past. Ray desperately looked around and saw a newsstand and magazine shop in the same strip mall as Oikawa's.

He had an hour to surreptitiously read enough magazine articles to make for a night's worth of interesting conversation. He walked in and the mustachioed Indian man behind the cash register called out, "Hey, the porn's in the back room."

"Uh, I'm not here for the, uh, porn," Ray said. "Just looking."

"Yeah, sure, buddy. Whatever. Don't make a mess."

It didn't seem to be worth an argument. Some photography magazines caught Ray's eye, but he wasn't sure how useful they'd be for actual conversation. Still, he had an hour. He flipped through quickly, but something caught his eye.

There was the symbol, photographed on a city street. It didn't look familiar. Then he saw another, and another. It was a story about what seemed to be a fairly big deal. The photos were making a splash. New York, Boston, Austin, Los Angeles, and Vegas. The photographer was Jenny Meyer.

"Holy shit," Ray said. He kept skimming through, looking for references to Jenny. The photos were taken from around the country. It was unclear if she was involved with the symbol or not. Photographer a virtual unknown and could not be reached for comment. Nothing else. He put the magazine under his arm to look at more later. He still had to get some conversation items.

He looked through the New Yorker hopefully, but the articles seemed to go on forever, and he put it back. Popular Mechanics was not nearly as interesting as he had remembered. The science magazines had mostly uninteresting theoretical stuff, but one pretty neat article about how dogs came to have such diversity within the species. He read the main points to remember for later. Wired had some neat stuff, but nothing worth talking about with a hot girl.

Ray had no idea what it was normal people talked about. He tried to remember what people talked about in TV and movies, but it had been a while, and he was actually pretty sure that wasn't a very accurate barometer for human communication. Politics were too depressing. The weather? The weather was a non-issue in Vegas: it was always hot and lame.

Ray got more and more nervous about what he was going to talk about. He had the symbol thing, which was her tattoo. She'd probably find that interesting. Maybe a couple of funny stories, like the time he and Ogami had convinced their high school newspaper to run a scathing editorial against itself. Or when he and Jenny would take turns pretending to be retarded in order to get special treatment at restaurants.

On second thought, bringing up Jenny might not be a great idea. The idea of her still made him very moody. And maybe Ogami was close to a point: sure, he didn't think of Jenny as a girlfriend, but maybe other girls were kind of skeeved out or intimidated by the friendship. The friendship was most likely over now, but then it would seem like he got dumped, when he clearly didn't. He was abandoned.

He looked at his watch and it was five after six. "Shit goddammit!" He remembered the magazine under his arm, and went up to the counter with it.

"You find everything you needed?" Mr. Mustache said.

Ray nodded.

"You sure? You didn't check out the back room."

"I know. I didn't come here for the back room. I'm late for a date, could you please hurry?" Ray hated lateness more than he hated anything else.

"Late, huh? Yeah, well, maybe you're gonna need that back room after all." Mr. Mustache laughed and rang Ray up. The magazine was pricier than he'd hoped, but, if nothing else, it would be a last goodbye to a good friend.

# CHAPTER TWENTY

He literally ran all the way over to Oikawa Sushi. This was a terrible idea for an out-of-shape thirty something smoker. He went in the restaurant and looked around, eyes wide with nervous fear. He saw no one. He feared that she had left because he was late. But he remembered that she was, after all, a girl. He'd not been on a date for quite a while, but he doubted that the entire female race started showing up on time in his absence.

He tried to slow his breathing and dabbed his sleeve on his forehead to wipe the sweat away. He was about to sniff his pits for B.O. when he heard, "About time you got here. I don't like being stood up."

Startled, he sprang around to see Cassandra. She had been around the corner waiting for him, apparently. Her hair was neatly pulled back and she'd put on a little bit of eye make-up. It made her almond-shaped eyes really stand out even more. Her lips were even nicer than he'd remembered. She wore an outfit that straddled the trendy/cute line perfectly. Ray looked at her and didn't even picture her naked. "Oh. Uh, sorry. I, uh, was actually a bit early, but then I—"

She laughed. "Don't worry, I just got here. I was afraid you'd left."

"No. No, I'm here."

"Yes, I can tell," she said. "You want to sit at the bar? I like it there."

"Yeah, sure," he said. He was used to sitting at bars. They just didn't usually have raw fish. A bar was a bar, though. They sat in the furthermost corner of the sushi bar. Behind it, across from them, was a middle-aged Japanese man. He was slightly chubby and had the smile of a man perfectly content with his life. He probably had a cute daughter and a dog that rarely barked.

"Konichiwa, Yoshi-san," Cassandra said, bowing slightly. Ray awkwardly bowed, too.

"Hello, Cass," Yoshi-san said. "Hello," he said again, bowing to Ray.

"Hi," Ray said, and he bowed again, feeling increasingly stupid. They took their seats.

"Do you have any preferences? I was going to get the omakase," Cassandra said.

"Um, I don't know what that is," Ray said, deciding faking it would not work at this point.

"Oh, it's when Yoshi-san chooses the fish and the cuts he recommends to us. The best of the best."

"Oh. Yeah, that sounds good. Less pressure on me for picking," Ray joked.

"Anything you really don't like? I don't like fish roe."

Ray thought about it. "Uh, do they have, like, octopus or anything like that? I don't think I want that."

Cassandra smiled. Yoshi-san came over, having seen the bright smile. "Yes?" he asked.

"Omakase, please, Yoshi-san. No roe, no octopus."

"Ah, very good. Very good," he replied, and began to work on cutting and preparing the fish. Ray watched for a moment but felt uncomfortable in the silence.

"My, uh, best friend's mom is Japanese," he said. "She mostly makes these really good noodle dishes and some nice fried chicken. Well, at least, when I was growing up she did. I dunno what she makes now."

"That's cool. I bet the home cooked stuff is great," she said. "I know I can't go to a Spanish restaurant. Nobody makes better *pernil* than my *abuela*."

"It's my mom's green beans that get me," Ray said. "Nobody makes green beans like that. I hate all green beans except hers, and I eat hers like candy."

Cassandra smiled. "Hey, I've been meaning to ask you. You said you were a private investigator. Was that a joke?"

"No, that's really my job." Ray took out his license. "See?"

"Wow, you really are," she said.

"Two kind of tuna," Yoshi-san said, placing down two pieces of sushi in front of each of them. "Fresh water, sea water," he pointed to make it clear.

Ray put his license away and watched Cassandra pick up the sea water tuna. Ray picked his up carefully with chopsticks and ate it in one bite. It was goddam fucking delicious. His eyes grew huge and he nodded his head and even made that "mmmmm" sound he never thought real people made outside of commercials. He swallowed.

"Good, huh?" Cassandra said.

"Oh, God, oh, Jesus. That's the best I've ever had, like, by far. Wow. Wow."

Yoshi-san smiled widely and his eyes crinkled up as he went to work on the next pieces.

While Ray was still reeling from the culinary orgasm, Cassandra prodded further. "So, what's it like, your job? I assume it's nothing like the books or TV shows or whatever."

"I don't really have cases or murders or femme fatales or anything. People come to me because they think someone's cheating on them. And they always are. I take pictures of it to help the divorce or whatever along. I don't ask questions and I don't make much money." He ate the second piece, having noticed Cassandra already doing likewise. "Oh, man," he spoke with his mouth full. "So goddam good. Jesus."

"So no wise-cracking sidekick? No eye for bizarre clues? No hard drinking?"

"Well, the hard drinking part I've got down," Ray said. "But that's more a holdover from art school, I think."

Cassandra laughed as Yoshi-san put down two orange pieces of fish for each of them. He explained they were two different kinds of salmon. Ray didn't wait this time, curious as to how good this could be. It was Real Goddam Good again. "Fuck, how'd you find this place?"

"Internet," Cassandra said. "Chowhound dot com. It's like a message board for people who like to find out-of-the-way great places to eat. I know, I'm a dork."

"Anybody who looks like you and who knows about a place like this can't be a dork," Ray said.

"Then why am I hanging out with you?" Cassandra asked, smiling.

"Nobody's perfect," Ray replied. He dove into the second salmon piece and his brain filled with endorphins. He no longer cared if he got laid. Well, he cared less. At that moment. He felt his muscles unclench. He was, finally, relaxed. Without a hint of booze.

The meal continued like this. The fish blew his mind so much that he forgot to worry about what to say. Relaxed, he actually conversed with Cassandra naturally. The wit that Ogami and Jenny had known so well actually got to come out and play. Ray was, of course, completely oblivious to this. He only knew that he felt good and he didn't want it to stop any time soon.

The check would have killed him at most times. It was the largest check he'd seen since people actually enjoyed paying for his meals. But he enjoyed paying for this one, and, again, thanks to Frankie, he had the money to do so. "So, uh," he said.

"Yeah," she said. "Let's get a drink. I want to see the hard drinking private dick in action."

"Play your cards right," Ray winked verbally. "Internet tell you about any great bars around here?"

"As a matter of fact, no," she said. "I deal with food. You're the drinker."

"Hmmm. I don't come around here that often."

"I, uh," she began, "don't mind going to your neighborhood. For drinks."

Ray was too relaxed to examine what that might mean, but days later he would, when the phrase came back to him. He didn't want to just take her to the Hole. It was fun, but she had gone all-out for dinner choice. "Hey, you ever been to the Big Top?"

"You mean Circus Circus?" she asked.

"Nope, Big Top. It's like the ghetto Circus Circus. But I know some folks that work there and there's usually some weird show there."

"Sounds fine to me, long as they have tequila. Do they have tequila?"

"They have tequila," Ray said. "Lots of tequila."

"Great. Let me call a car service. We'll arrive in style." She took out a phone and dialed up. Ray mused that it was somewhat impossible to arrive at the Big Top in style, but it would be fun trying nonetheless.

Dating was seeming to be much easier than he had remembered. Perhaps age mellowed it out in return for making the body not work right anymore. Ray was beginning to feel that it wasn't such a bad trade after all.

The taxi arrived promptly and they got in. Ray gave the Big Top's address and they were off. They weren't exactly traveling first class, but there was some class to it, which was more than Ray could usually say. "You said you liked Ansel Adams," he said. "Do you study photography?"

She shook her head. "No, I just like it as a bystander. I *am* studying, though. I'm not a career dancer or anything."

Ray felt embarrassed about the subject but also felt curious. "What are you studying?"

"Entertainment law, actually. Copyrights and that sort of thing."

"Huh," Ray said, like many people who have no idea what else to say.

"Yeah, it's not a very interesting job to talk about. And before you ask how I started dancing, it wasn't because I got molested or I'm a nympho or gay or any other cliché. My older sister did it and made some great money that she used to get her through hairdressing school. And the, uh, side jobs? Like where you were?"

Ray nodded, less comfortable. "I dunno how much he paid you, but that was the next two semesters for me. It was gross, but, hey, it's the only time I'll have to do it."

"Wow, that's cool, then. Frankie, he . . .he's weird. He's the slimiest piece of shit I've ever known, but he seems to do well by people he likes."

"Yeah, he's a weird one," she said. "I hate being around him, and I don't much care for what he stands for, but he's always been nice to me, I guess. How'd you meet him?"

"A dancer he knows hired me to catch her husband fucking around. He paid for it and then published some of the pictures in his little mag or whatever. Ever since then he's, uh, bought my, uh extra photos from time to time."

"Huh. I feel like everything I learn about him leads to a question I don't want answered," Cassandra said.

They had arrived at the Big Top. Ray paid the man and tipped him.

"I feel the same way," Ray said as they walked out.

"Interesting place," Cassandra said, pointing to the decorations.

"Just wait till you see the inside. If you brought sunglasses, now's the time." They walked in to a barrage of lights, flashing and steady both. The big time casinos kept a steady bright light in order to keep long-term gamblers unaware of changes in time of day. They

168

tried not to cause any seizures, though. The Big Top understood the confusing part, but got the rest pretty mixed up.

Clowns juggled near the entrance and in the distance a skinny hipster walked a tightrope high above the pit. "Jesus Christ, you weren't kidding," Cassandra said, shielding her eyes.

"You get used to it pretty quick. Or you drop to the floor and convulse for a while. You're not a convulser are you?"

"Not yet, at least," she said. "Let's start drinking and see if that helps."

They got seats at the bar. "Hey, Ray," Mark said. Mark was a bartender's bartender. He had a wide face that could smile and grimace equally impressively. He knew his drinks and he got them to you fast. His buyback policy was also a good one. Ray liked Mark and was happy to see him there. "Soph and O coming?"

Ray shook his head. "I dunno. Mark, this is Cassandra. She'd like a shot of your finest tequila."

Mark started pouring and smiled. "Pleased to meet you, Cassandra. I'm Mark and I'll be getting you drunk tonight. You're out with him, you'll need all the help you can get."

"It's Cass, actually, but thank you."

"Cass?" Ray said.

"Yeah. You don't listen too well, do you?"

Ray shrugged. "I guess not."

Mark set Cass up with a shot, some salt, and a lime. To Ray he gave a nice glass of bourbon. They clinked their glasses. "Rather have a bottle in front of me than a frontal lobotomy," Ray said and they began to drink.

# CHAPTER TWENTY-ONE

It was loud so they talked closely. Ray could feel her near him. Every movement seemed to be full of a million possibilities. Knees bumped and it might have meant something. Conversations varied from intimate to chit chat neither could have really cared about. It became about closeness, physically. It became about the almost-touch. Lips almost touching ears or faces or each other. Hands almost touching each other. Touching itself would be a heavy definite. It would be a yes or a no. At this point, the excitement of possibility was more appealing than any definites. Schrödinger's sexuality, they were electrified by the are-we-are-we-not intangible flirting going on underneath the surface of every movement and word.

Touching her shoulder wasn't about showing her something behind her, really. It was about the touch, about what it might or might not mean. Friendly pats lingered and eye contact was laser focused.

The master of ceremonies announced the next act, Anna the Anatomical Anomaly. Ray had met this girl before, but never actually been around to see her act.

"Oh, check this out," he said quietly into Cass' ear, hand lingering on her back to turn her around. "I've heard it's crazy."

Ray noticed how different Anna looked in her onstage regalia. Out of this context she had been a girl like many others he'd known. Pretty, in good shape, but not a head turner. In her tights, all made up, she became a different person. He had never been a fan of make-up, but it did wonders for Anna. Her eyes were emphasized and she looked mysterious and intense. It was funny: their only conversation had been about the difference between above-ground and normal pools. Not exactly interesting conversation.

She began her contortion act. She stretched her legs in seemingly inhuman ways. The music bordered on burlesque. There was a sexual air to this show of human flexibility. Ray knew better than to expect anything else from the Big Top. It had always exploited the primal sexual feeling that circuses and sideshows had aroused in men and women from the beginning.

Cass leaned back into him as they watched the show. On the surface, it was a woman doing weird shit with her body. But the booze, the food, the mood, it had all come together in a mix of instinctive arousal. Ray felt her shoulder blades against his chest and savored the feeling like a cokehead would a snort. He leaned forward to even up their heads and hers leaned back to meet him halfway. "Neat, huh?" he said.

They were long past the point where the content of the conversation was the point. They could both speak gibberish at this point and the message would still be the same: "I want to see you naked and then touch you and then we fuck."

"Jesus. I wonder if it hurts," Cass replied meaninglessly.

"I met her actually. She says it feels like a good workout. Kind of painful, but not like, you know, you think it would feel with your leg wrapped around you."

"You know her, huh?" Cass asked, mouth almost meeting Ray's. "You've got interesting friends."

"Compensation," he said, not flinching a hair, "for an uninteresting life." His hand was still on her, right above her hip. She was showing no problem with this. Schrödinger's flirting had made a decision, and now the question was "how far?"

They ordered more drinks and began to feel the hand of another world touching them. Some would say this was a feeling of inebriated inertia. Feelings felt while sober rolled along and snowballed as the booze piled up. Annoyed before drinking often leads to a drunken rage. Amused before leads to hysterical after. Attracted before leads to lust after.

But maybe it wasn't simple emotional physics. Emotional metaphysics: the suppressed ego of the intoxicated mind, the inflamed id, perhaps it was more akin to a trancelike state. Ray was a tipsy fakir, a foolish holy man capable of accessing higher power by sublimating the cultured self of society.

Regardless of the hows and wherefores, these two people didn't want to be at the bar anymore. "Do you wanna go?" Ray asked directly into her ear, hand on her elbow ever so slightly. She nodded and his hand wasn't on her elbow anymore, it was a taxi door. He was fairly certain he tipped well at the bar.

He told the driver his address. Cass sat very close to him in the back seat. They forwent seatbelts or any other safety devices. They were holding hands like horny middle schoolers, fingers stroking and constantly on the move.

They began half-hearted excuses, the last remnants of their societal selves.

"My place is a mess."

"I usually don't do this."

"This isn't just the booze."

Everything was truth, but none of the utterances were necessary. That telepathy Ray's brain had tried to develop in its most painful moments, it was coming to fruition. Cass and Ray were becoming shining examples of evolution, as they shed the individual and became Humanity itself.

Cass didn't even seem to notice the mess. Ray didn't fumble, didn't worry. They were close in his doorway. He poured drinks that neither needed. They sat on his futon and perhaps there was more small talk. If asked of it later on, neither would be certain. They would remember the closeness, the feeling of delayed inevitability. Like an infant holding in a large shit, there was a perverse delight in putting off what was obviously going to happen.

Ray looked at her eyes and her lips and felt in touch with the beauty of How Things Could Be. Every single shitty turn his life had taken had somehow helped lead him to right there, right then. The Approaching Now of Forever. They sat and suddenly Ray spurted, "Is it OK if I kiss you?"

"Jesus, about time. I was afraid my signals were broken." He leaned in and he kissed her once very softly. He didn't pull away, instead, kissing her again, harder. Lips were bit, grips got tighter.

"Is there anything I can do for you?" Ray wanted to please her.

"Take off your shirt." As it was covering his head he felt her undo his pants and start to suck his dick. He jerked his shirt the rest of the way off, needing to see this happen. It looked amazing, her streaked hair bobbing slowly on him. Ray was very glad that he had jerked off earlier, as he felt close to spurting already. She looked up at him with large brown eyes and he felt himself start to come.

"Uhhh, no, I'm gonna—" Ray said, pulling out of her mouth. She looked at him questioningly. "I don't want to, uh, end so fast," he said.

"Me neither," she said. "My turn." She took off her shirt and threw it to the floor. Ray fumbled with her pants, but they were tight around the ass and she helped him remove them. Her panties were electric blue and lacy, and he was careful not to rip them in his excitement. He kissed her legs and began to eat her out with gusto.

It was like riding a bicycle: he didn't quite forget how, but it was tough to remember how to do it well. He knew he wasn't setting any records or giving her a Penthouse moment, but Ray felt like he did the work of an accomplished journeyman. When her body shook and she cried out and grabbed his head, he felt that rare pleasure of a job well done.

His head was clearer now, the adrenaline and testosterone bullying the alcohol out of control. "Do you have a condom?" she asked and he nodded. He walked over to a little case where he kept condoms and opened it for the first time in longer than he cared to remember. He put it on and felt like Arthur retrieving the sword from the stone. He was back, he was king, and he was going to fuck.

They fucked and he liked it. They started in missionary, which he had never thought of as boring. Nothing boring about watching her pretty face as they fucked. But she pushed him off at one point and got on her knees. "From behind," she said, and it wasn't a request.

Ray fumbled to get in, but her hand pulled him in tightly. He watched her look back at him and just stared at her eyes. He grasped her tits joyfully, stroked her entire body, taking in every sight. He ran his finger over her tattoo of that symbol and she began to come again, one of her own hands helping her out. It was too much for Ray and he finished with a loud yelp.

He knew he must have been quite loud for much of the time, as his throat was raw with exertion. He rolled away from her and nearly forgot to take the full condom off. He spilled a bit of himself onto his futon but didn't care too much.

"Jesus," he said. He smiled at her and kissed her as she lay on his bed. They both lay there silently, unaware of the passage of time or the rest of the world. Ray became unaware of everything except a satisfied, warm calm that covered him like a cushion fort built on a rainy day.

# CHAPTER TWENTY-TWO

His next awareness was of the futon shaking. Cass was getting up. "Whereyou—" he slurred sleepily.

"Gotta pee," she said, and his sudden jitters were calmed. He was embarrassed that he'd fallen asleep like the punch line of a badly-written sitcom. Surely she'd understand that it was kind of a compliment. Ray was rationalizing like a motherfucker.

When she came back she smiled. "Your bathroom smells weird. Are you OK?"

"Huh?" Ray asked needlessly. "Oh, yeah. That's, uh, photo chemicals. I develop in there. I kind of get used to it, sorry."

She laughed. "Hey, that's a fine explanation. I was afraid you made that smell yourself. That would be some seriously fucked up shit there, literally."

"Sorry that I fell asleep," Ray couldn't escape his guilt. "I, it was—"

"Don't sweat it, I did too. Sex is a lot of work when you mean it."

This put Ray's guilt alarms on standby. "That was, uh, that was really good," he said. The natural flow of inebriated conversation had fallen to the wayside and the unnatural awkwardness of post-fucking conversation had taken over.

Cass smiled graciously. "Thanks. I was a little worried when you almost came right out of the gate, but you redeemed yourself pretty well." Ray decided to try to take this as a compliment.

He looked at the time and it was well past night and headed straight for morning. "Uh, do you want to, uh, stay here? My place isn't great, but it's pretty late out."

"Reminds me of the year I lived in a dorm," she said. "Except there were four of us to account for this amount of mess."

"I'm very productive when it comes to mess," Ray said as he always did when people commented on the state of his apartment. It was a tired joke, but Cass was a new recipient. Ray took time to look at her naked body. He liked it even more than the first time he had seen it. The curves were right where they needed to be, full without being "Reubenesque." Her skin was smooth, almost as if it had been powdered beforehand. He wanted to grab her all over. "That tattoo," he said, looking at it. "I, uh, a friend of mine took pictures of it. Of something like it." He pulled the magazine out of a bag and stood up to show her. "See, this article? She, uh, she took all these photos."

"Who?" Cass said, leafing through the magazine.

"Jenny. Jenny Meyers. She's a good friend of mine. Or, uh, was. I dunno."

Cass looked at him, confused.

"I mean, I haven't heard from her in a while. Months. So, uh, I guess she's not my friend anymore or something." He was drowning and he knew it but he kept diving further down, looking for some pearl of an explanation. He decided to go for distraction.

"So, uh, what is it? That symbol, I mean."

She looked around the apartment and picked up some of her clothes. "I dunno, I just thought it looked cool."

"Oh," Ray said. Something seemed wrong.

"Thanks for the, uh, offer of hospitality," she said. "That's really sweet of you. But I have to go home. I've got, uh, too many errands to run tomorrow."

"Oh, uh, OK." Ray knew he shouldn't feel rejected. He'd probably rather stay at her place than here, too. He watched her get dressed and felt aroused again, even though it would be a while before he could get a hard-on again.

She called herself a cab and he got dressed himself, suddenly feeling very vulnerable and stupid while naked. He inwardly listed a dozen things he should probably say, though naught but cliché emerged from his lips. "I had a really great time tonight."

She looked at him and smiled. "I did too, Ray."

"Can I give you a call sometime?" he asked shakily.

She kept the smile and nodded. "Yeah, of course you can. What, you think I'm a whore or something?"

"No no no! No, I don't!" Ray said.

Her smile grew and he felt at ease again. His calmness seemed to be directly proportional to the size of her smile. Her teeth shot lasers that evaporated unease. "I know you don't, Ray. Calm down."

So he calmed down.

When she left, it was the kind of leaving that hurt and felt great at the same time. Like looking at a too-bright sunset, there was a beauty in the stinging. After watching her cab turn the corner and standing there a few more moments, Ray returned to bed and fell quickly to sleep.

The next morning he dialed Ogami before even getting out of bed.

"Konichiwa, motherfucker. You've reached Ogami Burroughs. Leave all love letters, death threats, and encoded messages at the beep."

"Hey, HomO," Ray said. "It's me. You gotta call me. I went out with Cassandra last night and it was great. Great. You have to call me. Bye."

Ray showered happily, and the water temperature didn't bother him a whit. His stomach was hungry and he was going to reward it with good food. His hangover was slight to the point of being inconsequential. He felt like walking the whole way to the Greasy Spoon, but knew that was a horrible idea in practice. He caught the bus and even gave a couple dollars to a beggar on the sidewalk.

Ray, like so many people, was a much nicer person when he was actively fucking. He was more caring when he had evidence that more people cared. Ray thought of himself as an individualist, but really tended to act as those around him acted.

He took his booth and ran his hands over the Formica table. The sun was impressive and he quite realized what an idiot he was being. *'One night of sex and you're all birdies and kittens and happiness,'* he thought. *'You're a pathetic one, Ray Brautigan.'* His self-awareness was not a self-destruction, though he did stop himself from whistling.

Tammy came over, uniform neat as ever. "Hey, Hun. What'll you have?"

"Salami, egg, and bacon on a roll," he said.

"Small tomato juice and large OJ?" she asked.

"Yeah!" Ray said with excessive, but genuine enthusiasm. This was an important step in becoming a "regular." A waitress recognized his order. Ray often ordered the same thing over and over again. This wasn't because he was unadventurous or uncreative. It was both because he really liked the item more than the others on the menu and he hoped it would help him stay in the waitress' or waiter's mind. So he had regular drinks, regular sandwiches, regular pasta . . .he thought that if he were consistent, people would at least remember him for that.

Service was fast and the sandwich perfect. Ray wondered if the Greasy Spoon was ever mentioned on that website Cass had talked about. He had been an internet fiend when he could afford the computer and the connection, but ultimately it was no better use of his time than watching hours upon hours of bad television. The access to porn was hard to beat, though. He made a mental note to ask her about it.

He wondered when he should call her. He had heard and remembered all the supposed rules as to dating. They all seemed retardedly arbitrary. He knew that calling her immediately was fucking stupid and desperate, but a three day or four day waiting seemed equally stupid. Truth was he wanted to call her right then and there, but wasn't quite ignorant enough to follow through.

Trouble was, he had nothing else to do for the entire day. Ample time and little activity had always proved to be a danger for Ray Brautigan. He could waste the day away boozing, and, yes, there was an appeal to that. Or he could go out and maybe buy something with his new money, but Ray couldn't think of anything he could afford that he really needed.

The thought of the internet had put a seed into his head. He thought he'd go to that Chowhound site and look up the Greasy Spoon, or maybe a new place he could surprise Cass with on their next date. He knew of an internet café he used when he needed to do some research on a client. Libraries and halls of records weren't so necessary to an investigator now that Google was around.

# CHAPTER TWENTY-THREE

Ray caught a bus that took him near the Information Lounge and was there before two. He found the food website that Cass had liked and spent a while looking things up. Oikawa Sushi had pretty crazy good reviews, and everyone recommended Yoshi-san, the chef they'd had. The Hole in the Wall Bar was actually listed, too, in the section for dive bars. Ray felt proud that his favorite place merited a mention. He recognized several other joints, too.

There was no mention of the Greasy Spoon, so Ray signed up to be able to post one himself. He wondered if Cass would see it before seeing him.

He had some time to kill afterwards, so he decided to once again Google himself. He had a rare enough name that most internet mentions of a Ray Brautigan were actually him. There was still not much of note. A couple of old pages referring to gallery shows he'd done. Posts from message boards. Weird lists of names that seemed to be spam or something. Nothing new.

He looked up Ogami and noticed a couple of new fan pages since the last time he'd done this. They were clearly from teenage girls, and their devotion was somewhere between adorable and terrifying. Teenage girls reminded Ray of Amy. He thought about calling her about last night, but two things stopped him. First, it seemed a little awkward, telling one crush about another. Ray then realized he had admitted to himself that he had a crush on Amy. He chided himself for trying to deny it. Having a crush didn't mean he was a pedophile or was even going to act on it. She was a pretty, fun girl. Of course he had a crush on her.

But the other reason he didn't call her was a more obvious one. She was at school. She shook his head and laughed that he had a friend he couldn't call because she was in school. Ray's life never ceased to take weird turns that surprised even him. He looked her up on Google and found some local high school soccer stats. He didn't know that she played soccer. It was funny, he'd always liked girls that played soccer. Amazing calves. There were other pages with her name on Friendster and Myspace, which both seemed to be some kind of weird list of people that you know. Ray considered making an account for himself, but that was just his old internet addiction taking hold again.

He looked up Cassandra Reyes, feeling a little guilty. It wasn't stalking, it was research. And, frankly, he liked her and wanted to see her or read about her if he couldn't be around her. His worry was in vain, as there were no references to her name that seemed to actually be about her.

He stared at the screen. He typed "Jenny Meyers" into the search box, but didn't press enter. He told himself that maybe he'd find out something else about that damn symbol that seemed to be everywhere.

He was surprised to see that no pages had any reference to Jenny Meyers. He had looked her up before, the last time he was at a computer, and she had quite a few references. There were even a couple of pages about her work. That they didn't exist anymore seemed a little weird. Perhaps they'd just stopped existing. Ray had made a web page in college about Ogami's band, and it didn't exist anymore, so maybe it wasn't so weird after all.

He still wanted to learn more about the symbol but was at a loss as to how to do so. He knew full well that typing in "weird symbol" wasn't going to do much good for anyone. He went back up to the counter where you paid for the service. There was a nerd there that looked like the kind of guy that might know how to do it.

"Hey, Bill," Ray said, reading the nametag "I'm, uh, I want to look up about a symbol I've seen painted places. But, uh, I'm not sure how. Like I know what it looks like, but I don't know what it's called."

"Mr. Carter to you," the nerd said. Ray fought back the tiny bully that lived deep within him. "So what do you need from me?"

Sometimes people that were shat upon socially their whole lives deserved it. Not every nerd was a prince under the thick glasses. Many were annoying fucks that asked every time they spoke for every bully around to kick their ass. And when these nerds found themselves in a position of power, watch out. They liked nothing more than exacting revenge upon the world that treated them the way they begged to be treated. They reveled in a sense of superiority that would put most NBA players to shame.

Worse still, you just have to sit there and take it. If you need their services, you have to let them gloat and whinny and fellate their own shitty nerd ego. Ray sat there and took it. "I was wondering if you could help me, if you knew a way to look it up. I'd really appreciate it."

"So you want me to leave my desk and help you look up some illegal symbol you saw painted somewhere? Is that it? You want the internet to magically teach you all about your little gang sign?"

There were dozens of things that Ray wanted to say at this point, but none of them would have gotten good results. "Yes," he said instead. "I would really appreciate it, please."

"Why the hell should I waste my time with that?"

Ray had answers. Many answers. "So that I don't kick your ass, nerd," was one of them. "Because it's your goddam job, nerd," was a more reasonable one. He decided against these first two impulses and went for an old standby Ogami's dad had taught him when he first started digging into other people's business. He took a twenty dollar bill out of his wallet and placed it on the counter. "That's why," he said.

Maybe the nerd looked at the bill and saw a Star Wars DVD or some action figures or a lap dance. All that matters is that he took it and went to help Ray.

"I have a hacker friend," the nerd said, "who's into tagging. He knows this site where the good stuff gets listed, publicized, and discussed. Password protected, but I can get you in."

Sometimes the obnoxiousness came hand in hand with usefulness. The nerd typed as quickly as his chubby fingers could type and soon Ray was at a website with lots of graffiti from around the world indexed and pictured. "Thanks," he said and even kind of meant it.

A lot of the site was various names and nicknames of "taggers." It all looked kind of similar. There were some murals that were truly impressive. Some of the rural areas had some kids that were trying their best, but just weren't very good. Ray looked and looked, almost forgetting why he had started in the first place. But then he found the "unknown artists" section. Pictures were posted and sometimes pieces' creators took credit. Or someone tried to take credit. Some pieces were under dispute, sometimes pretty hotly.     Ray couldn't help but think these were just another breed of nerd, arguing over graffiti instead of Star Trek.

But there it was, a simple picture at first, of that "A" and star. This led to picture after picture, all from different places, from all over the country. Some of the photos were recognizably Jenny's seen in the magazine. But most were clearly home photos from the various kids posting on the site. Nobody knew who made them or what they

y

185

meant, but theories abounded, from secret government agency to militia to new gang to a new anonymous artist on the level of Basquiat or Neckface.

There was no mention of it as a tattoo.

"Hey, can I print this?" Ray called out.

"It's not my paper," the nerd affirmed. "Knock yourself out."

Ray printed and went up to pay the nerd, who was looking at his printed pages. "What's the big deal?" he asked.

"Don't know," Ray said. "Girls," he added.

"Shyeah, right," the nerd said, giving Ray his change.

Ray went home with his new materials in hand and on the way received a phone call. "Brautigan," he answered.

"Hey, Gay." It was Ogami. "What's with the message?"

"Yeah, hey, what you doing?" Even though they could talk with no self-consciousness, talking on the phone about feelings was for women. Men did it over drinks.

"Just finished practice. Got nothing till the band practices tonight."

"Meet me at the Hole," Ray said.

"Smell ya later," Ogami replied and hung up. When arranging a meeting with a woman or a client, Ray had to be very sure to include times, exact locations, and back-up spots. With Ogami, this was not necessary. He would be there, he would be there soon, and he would be in the same place he usually was.

And he was: playing video poker. A wad of bills sat on top of the screen as O played away. As Ray was about to sit, Ogami said, "I knew you were there. I think my Japanese Ninja Sense might finally be kicking in."

"Or I'm real loud," Ray said. Ogami flipped him a friendly bird.

"What's up, fucker? I'm on a streak here. I've won five bucks."

"Oooh, five bucks. Time to buy that swimming pool for the summer house."

Ogami looked up for the first time. "You're awfully lively today. You haven't been—HOLY SHIT YOU GOT LAID DIDN'T YOU?!" Ray nodded. "Oh, man. You said it went great, but I figured you meant relatively. Not objectively great. Wow, man, congrats."

"Thanks. She's really cool, too. I'm going to call her soon."

"You're not following some dumbass rule as to when to call her are you? I called Soph back the day after our first date. I just had to, you know?"

"Yeah, I know. Fuck. It's cool."

"What's she do?" Ogami asked, eyes back on his game.

"Uh, well, she's studying entertainment law. Something about copyrights or something."

"College girl? Living off dad's money?"

"Uh, no. She also, uh, dances."

Ogami looked back up. "You're dating a stripper? You fucked a stripper?"

"Well, I went out with her, and, yeah, we fucked. But she's not, like, a stripper stripper."

"Dude, I knew you had it in you. Wait, let me ask you. Is she clean? Did she have a smell?"

Ray nearly coughed up his bourbon from choking. "Jesus! Yeah, she's fine! No smell. Not that I could tell or anything."

"OK, just checking. Cause, you know, some strippers . . .YES! Five more dollars! Eat it, Brautigan!"

"You better cash out while you're ahead," Ray said. He'd lived in Vegas a long time, but it didn't take long to teach him that gambling was a fool's game. It wasn't just that he had bad luck (he did), the entire system was designed to take people's money. That's fine for the tour-ons, but locals should know better.

Ogami, on the other hand, was just lucky. "Yeah, guess you're right. Hey, what's with all the paper? You studying something?"

"It's that symbol," Ray said, pointing to one printed-out photo. "The one we found in Jenny's place." Ogami looked at it warily. "It's apparently some big graffiti mystery. Nobody knows what it is or who did it."

"Ray. You got a girl. Don't fuck this up with this Jenny shit."

"No, no. Cass, she's got this tattooed on her back."

"Oh, yeah, that's right." Ogami said, looking more deeply at the papers now.

"Yeah, weird, huh?"

Ogami nodded. "Hey, let me use my copious winnings to buy us some more magic fire water."

Ray sat back and looked around as his friend purchased more booze. It was fairly empty for middle afternoon in Las Vegas. Some people would think that in a city where bars were open twenty-four hours a day, the locals would have gotten tired of it after a few years. These people do not understand the appeal of booze, and probably hate Santa Claus as well.

Ray and Ogami shared a few drinks, practicing rare moderation. Ray halfway noticed that when it was just the two of them, neither boozed too hard. They spent too much time talking and laughing to really get much of a drink on in a short period of time. After a while, the two parted, Ogami on his way to band practice, and Ray home in a happy buzz-contentment combination.

# CHAPTER TWENTY-FOUR

Around five, Ray's phone rang again. He quickly picked it up, hoping to hear Cassandra. "Hey, dork, it's Amy," he heard instead.

"Oh," he replied. He realized he sounded disappointed, so he added, "Hey! How are you?"

"I'm fine, Rainbow Sunshine. What got into you?"

"Uh, I dunno. Just happy, I guess."

"Will wonders never cease," she said. "Anyway, what are you doing tonight?"

"I dunno," Ray felt an immediate quandary. He enjoyed Amy's company, he enjoyed it quite a bit. But it often felt weird to him. He had come to terms with the fact that he wanted to fuck a teenage girl, mostly by telling himself that he never would. But "never" is a very tough word, especially when people go drinking.

On the other hand, he didn't have any plans. "What's going on?" he asked finally.

"I'm supposed to go to this open mic poetry thing. But I'm really afraid it's going to be lame. I need company."

"Uh, is this, uh, a school thing?" Ray asked. It was one thing hanging out with one mature seventeen-year-old. A gaggle of them seemed like a more probable disaster than Hitler on roller skates.

"No. This guy I know invited me. He's supposed to read and I didn't want to say no."

"How old is this guy?"

"Thirty-two," she said.

"Jesus, do you have ANY friends your own age?"

"Didn't see you complaining the other night," she teased. "Come on! I'll let you buy me some drinks!"

"Wow, that's a big motivator for me. I get to buy you drinks, huh? Wow, I can't see how I could possibly refuse that."

"You know it's true," she said. Ray had to admit, the evening sounded like possible fun. Drinks, making fun of lame poets, and a cool girl. There was a twitch of irrational guilt, Ray recognized it. The guilt of cheating on someone you don't really have. But he wasn't going to sleep with Amy. It wasn't a date. Ray had always had female friends, and even if Jenny had disappeared — abandoned him — then there was no reason for this not to continue.

"Yeah, sure, why not." Amy gave Ray instructions as where and when to meet. "I don't have to, uh, dress up or anything do I?" Ray imagined a cartoon of poets in black garb and berets. Ray didn't own a beret.

"No, dork. Normal clothes are fine. As long as they smell less than you usually do."

"Hey!" Ray found himself extra offended because he couldn't tell if she was joking or not. "Just for that, I'm gonna rub your drinks in my armpits while you're not looking."

"Ew!" Amy screamed through the phone. "I don't know if I like you this feisty."

"Get used to it," he said. "See you there." He smiled at the phone and felt in charge of his life. He boiled up some hot dogs to sate his hunger and thought about how much one night can change things.

He wanted to call Cass. He wanted so badly to forget any advice he'd heard about not calling a girl too soon. But he also remembered that girls wanted to be called the day after they had sex. It was a courtesy thing, a "Yes, I'm still interested in what you have to say when you're not screaming an orgasm."

So he was going to call her. But what if she asked about that night? He was supposed to hang out with Amy. And he had no idea how she'd feel about him going out drinking with an underage girl a night after they first slept together.

He'd play it off as nothing, he decided. A former client that still needed some help. Kind of a friend. Would he be calling Cass if he were really interested in this other girl?

Was he?

He put that out of his mind. He had to call Cass. He wanted to talk to her. And maybe she'd have him come by after the dumb poetry thing. He picked up his phone and dialed.

It rang. It rang. A click as it picked up. "We're sorry," an automated voice began, "we cannot connect you to that number as dialed. Please hang up and try again. Thank you."

Ray looked at his phone. He was pretty sure that he had correctly entered Cassandra's number, but dumber shit had happened. He went to his call log and directly redialed the number where he'd first contacted her.

"We're sorry, we cannot connect you to that number as dialed. Please hang up and try again. Thank you."

'Shit,' Ray thought. 'Must be my connection. I'll try again later.' But Ray didn't really have that kind of patience at that moment, so he walked outside of his apartment, almost into the street. His phone was showing great reception. He tried again, redialing by hand the number he had written down when Frankie told him.

He hung up after hearing the "We're sorry," again.

"Fuck! Shit motherfucker!" Ray was oblivious to proper outside public behavior. Thankfully, he was still in the ghetto of Las Vegas, where propriety was a rather lenient concept. He decided to see if his phone was fucked up again and called Ogami.

"Konichiwa, motherfucker. You've reached Ogami Burroughs. Leave all love letters, death threats, and encoded messages at the beep."

"Fuck," Ray said into the phone. Then he remembered that he was leaving a message. "Shit. I think something's wrong. Cass' phone is disconnected or something. Uh, you're at practice. I'll talk to you later."

Ray stood on the sidewalk staring at his phone. *'Maybe her phone is getting bad reception,'* he thought. *'Shit, it's probably something simple like that.'* Ray went back into his apartment and tried to be calm. It didn't work too well so he tried a slug of bourbon. *'Time to get better bourbon,'* he thought.

He looked through the computer print-outs again. That symbol, that damn symbol. Ray believed in coincidences. In fact, his life often centered around them. But that was the very thing: the coincidences always meant something. It was random chance that added up to something else. Art from chaos.

There were two choices: either the women in his life were all abandoning him or something was going on with that goddam symbol. Jenny leaves her apartment in a weird rush, with that symbol on her floor and wall. Jenny takes pictures of it, gets published, isn't around to be contacted. That wasn't like her. She'd usually have loved to get an interview, if only to make inappropriate remarks. Then Ray got beat up right by one of the damn things. And when he asks Cassandra about it, she leaves and now her phone doesn't work.

He wanted to hash this out with someone; Ogami's mom apparently did much of the connect-the-dots work when Ogami's dad was dicking. But Ogami thought this was just a weird fixation on Jenny. And he may have been right, but Ray wanted a fresh perspective. His options were limited. Amy, Frankie, and Soph limited, and none of them seemed right. Amy didn't know him well enough, he didn't trust Frankie and Soph . . .what, he was going to go hang out with his friend's girl?

Ray mulled it over, calming down. It was possible that her phone was just out of service or batteries or something. He'd go out with Amy and try calling Cass later. Maybe he'd hash things out with Amy anyway. He had wanted a fresh perspective, so someone who didn't know him for years might be able to give it.

He took another slug of bourbon and smoked a cigarette. He chuckled to himself at his overreaction. Ogami would give him such hell if he ever found out.

If he was overreacting.

Another big pull of cheap bourbon and he didn't care. Only a little bit left. He killed the plastic jug and promised himself to buy something better than this rotgut. He looked at his clock and knew it was time to go meet Amy. He was drunker than he'd planned on being, but that was probably only going to help him at an open mic poetry night.

# CHAPTER TWENTY FIVE

When Ray arrived, Amy was actually already there. It helped that the busses were fucked and he was twenty minutes late. She was wearing a cute little floral print dress. It wasn't low cut but the skin above her chest looked firm and smooth. "You look nice," he said.

Amy grabbed her nose in mock disgust. "You got started early. I don't blame you." She pulled out a pewter flask. "So did I. Come on. Let's do this."

They walked in and sat on a rather cushy sofa. Ray wasn't the oldest man in the building. He was, in fact, square in the middle, it seemed. There were creepy old guys, and lame-ass looking young guys. He wondered where this put him.

Amy nudged him and pointed to a guy around his own age with a slightly-more-receding hairline but better clothes. "That's Scott," she said. "He's the one that invited me here."

"Should you, uh, be over there with him?"

"Ew! No!" Amy said. "Yuck. No, I shouldn't. He's kind of creepy. I don't know why I agreed to come here. I guess I thought it'd be funny."

"Let's hope so," Ray said. He went and bought a couple drinks and came back. "I, uh, want to talk to you, uh, when we can."

Amy raised a thin brown eyebrow at him. "What kind of talk?"

"Just . . .just some weird shit going on in my life, and I want another perspective."

"Oh, whew. OK. Listen, if — when this gets unbearable, let's head out and talk. Cheers."

Amy held her glass high. "Clinky clinky, drinky drinky."

"Welcome," a smarmy MC announced into the mic. "Welcome. We've got some great poets lined up tonight. I see Scott out there, hey Scott. I see Cristen. Yeah, this is going to be great. But first up, I'd like to read something myself."

"Uh-oh," Ray said, a bit too loud.

"This first piece is called 'Special Time with Daddy.'"

Ray immediately sunk his head into his hands. Amy failed to stifle a snicker. She played it off like she was choking on her Scotch, but few would buy it. "Ray!" she whisper-screamed. "Finish your drink, we're getting out of here."

Ray sat straight up, chugged the rest of his bourbon, and fled the scene he was rapidly making. Once outside, the two burst into peals of laughter, like that morning's first piss after a drunken night.

"Oh, fuck. Thanks. I would not have lasted long in there. Is, uh, your friend going to be pissed?"

"Yeah," Amy said. "But who gives a shit? Besides, he can't stay mad at me. I'm a cute girl."

"You guys have a certain power," Ray admitted. "Let's go to the Hole."

Amy stared at him for a second. "Oh, oh, oh! The bar. Yeah, let's go. " They got a car and drank from Amy's flask along the way. They took turns reciting what they thought the MC's poem might have been to increasing fits of laughter.

At the Hole, Ray filled Amy in over their respective favorite whiskeys. It was a long story, told pretty much from the beginning. How he met Jenny, how he had been interested in her, how he ultimately decided that they'd make better friends than failed lovers.

"Bullshit," Amy said. "I've heard that one before."

"What?" Ray asked.

"Nothing. Go on."

Ray hated not getting and answer, but knew better than to keep trying. He finished talking about Jenny. The sort of times they'd had, the sort of people they were.

"You actually, you remind me of her. It's one of the things that kind of fucked with me when we first met. That and the jailbait thing."

Amy shot him a finger. "I'm perfectly legal, I'll have you know."

"Anyway, like I said, she'd fall out of touch while she was working, that was no problem. She traveled and shit. But it's been over three months now since I've heard from her. And when I went to her place, she had moved out, hastily, and not all the way. And this symbol, this damn symbol . . ." Ray drew it on a napkin. He explained everywhere he had seen it, leaving Cassandra out for the time being. That still felt like something he shouldn't talk about in front of Amy.

"I dunno, Ray," Amy said. "Yeah, that's kind of weird, but not a big deal. So there's a new thing going around, some De La Guarda dipshit painting something that makes no sense everywhere. It's not really suspicious."

Ray knew then that he couldn't leave Cassandra out. She was the part that made it more than coincidence. She was the step too far and Amy was still on the other side of the line. That is, if her line really was disconnected.

"Hey, uh, I have to make a phone call," Ray said suddenly. "I'll, uh, be right back. I want to talk more."

"Blah blah blah blah blah," Amy said, making her hand into a talky puppet.

Ray walked out of the bar and took his phone out of his pocket. He began to hate the damn thing more than ever before. He saw it as the source of all these recent troubles. For a moment, he wanted to throw it into the street and say "Fuck you" to the whole thing.

But if there was a chance that Jenny hadn't left his ass in the grime and dust, if she actually was mixed up in some sort of trouble, well, Ray had done a lot of shitty things in his life, but he'd never left a friend needing. And now was no time to start. He dialed Cassandra's number one more time, wanting desperately for her to answer, or at least her answering machine. If she answered, everything was fine, even if she never wanted to see him again. He pressed "send" and put the phone to his year.

He jerked his head away as it started ringing loudly. "Goddammit," he said. Someone was calling him. He mashed the buttons, trying to remember how to pick up another line. Maybe this was Cass calling. Or even Jenny.

"Hello?" he said, to no answer. "Hello?" The phone continued to loudly ring in his ear. He tried pressing the "send" button again, always wary that it wasn't the right one. "Hello?" he repeated desperately.

"Ray Brautigan my boy! It is me, Frankie!" Curses flew through Ray's head like coyotes chasing roadrunners.

"Yeah, hi, Frankie, I actually —"

"So, you must tell me, my boy! Did you call beautiful Cassandra? I think you did!"

"Yeah, I did. I'm actually—"

"Did you see her? Tell me if you saw her! Did you have a date to remember?"

"Yes," Ray sighed. "We went out. I'm actually trying to call her right now."

"You call her again so soon? You break date rules! Oh! I know! You had fuck action! Fuck action!"

"Frankie, goddammit, I was actually dialing her number when you called. I, uh, need to—"

"My boy Ray Brautigan, I knew it. He is fuck action king of Las Vegas! This is great news! Maybe we have you two do special photo spread? I have been thinking of publishing actual magazine, making the real money! You two—"

"Frankie! I'm sorry, I am, but I'm really, really busy now. I will talk to you later, OK?"

"It is OK, it is OK. Why talk to fat old man when beautiful fuck babes want your fuck action all the time?" Frankie laughed and it almost calmed Ray. "We will talk later, my boy. Be careful and get no diseases on your cock! Keep fucking them bitches!"

"Yeah, bye," Ray said, frustration almost complete. He hated call waiting to begin with, and it always seemed to be at inopportune moments. This was just the worst example he'd had. It seemed even more difficult to redial Cassandra's number, even though he only had to press one button twice. He wondered if Truman felt the same way when bombing Japan, and then felt the stupidest he'd felt in ages for wondering that.

He pressed, he pressed.

# CHAPTER TWENTY-SIX

"Well?" Amy asked. "What's going on? You look like shit."

Ray threw back the rest of his bourbon and went to get another round before answering. He took another big slug after sitting down.

"Jesus, Ray. Did you get drafted? Are you breaking up with me?"

Ray nearly coughed up his bourbon at that one. "What?"

"Joke. Meant to make people laugh. Jesus, you're uptight tonight. You need to get laid."

"No, I don't," Ray said. "Look, there's more to the story. There was, there is a girl. I met her at a, uh, photo shoot."

"A model? Ooooo!" Amy teased.

Ray loosened a bit. "Yeah. We went out last night and, uh, had a really good time. Really. It was pretty awesome."

"OK, so you did get laid," Amy said. Was her reply terse? "What's this got to do with anything else?"

"Well, that symbol, this symbol," Ray said, pointing again to the napkin, "was tattooed on her."

"OK, so she's really hip and trendy or something. So?"

"Well, I asked her about it and she clammed up, got dressed, and left."

"Ooookay, yeah, that's a little weird, but maybe she's just sensitive about it?"

Ray drank more bourbon. "And I called her today and her line is disconnected."

"Maybe you just had a bad connection," Amy suggested. Ray shook his head.

"I've tried all over. I just tried again. That was the last test. All day, nothing. Something's going on, Amy. It has to be. This is a coincidence that means something. It's not just that these women are dumping me without saying goodbye. Something's going on."

Ray took another big drink. "This symbol, it has something to do with it."

They sat there in silence for a while, well, relative silence. It was still a dive bar after all. The din of drunken small talk, awkward come-ons, and gnashings of teeth was still there, but to Ray they seemed to fade away.

"OK," Amy said finally. "Let's figure out what it means."

"Huh?" Ray said. Though he had tried to hope, he did not expect an open reaction from anyone. It was just too stupid and crazy. The obvious answer was that these people just got tired of him and everything else was coincidence. But Ray seemed hell-bent on cutting himself with Occam 's razor.

"I said 'Let's figure out what it means,'" Amy repeated. "That would help us figure out what's going on, right? You're afraid that maybe these folks are in danger or endangering someone else. I think you want to know the truth. We'll have to look for it."

"Right," Ray said, stunned. "Right. I just, well, I just don't know how to do that."

"You're the detective! What do you usually do?"

"Uh, you know. Follow people around. Take pictures of them. Uh, look them up on the internet."

"What about that site you said you saw the symbol on? It's a message board, right? Maybe you could post on it or check what other people have said since you last checked. Shit happens fast on the internet."

Ray felt a kind of enthusiasm his life so rarely lacked in these days begging to bubble up in his rotted gut. "Yeah. We could go back to that internet café and check that out again."

After a sip of Scotch, Amy asked, "What are we waiting for? An engraved invitation?"

Ray pounded the rest of his drink back. "Let's roll," he said with a wink. Amy finished her drink and they left the Hole. "It's just down this way about ten blocks," Ray said. "We could even walk."

"Listen to Mr. Exercise here. Let's do it." They began to walk and Amy took a cigarette out. "Smoke?"

Ray took his own out. "I'm good." He lit Amy and then himself as they walked.

"I thought you said your detective stuff was never like this."

"It isn't," Ray said. "It might not be now. Maybe I am being paranoid about being a loser. But it doesn't hurt to look into it. Listen," Ray said, wondering how to continue. "Thanks for this. For listening, and for trying. I, uh, I really appreciate it."

"Psssh," Amy waved him off. "It beats listening to MC Lame-ass rhyming about his daddy."

They were three blocks away from the café when they realized something was going on. "Shit," Ray said. "Must have been a big fire." Firetrucks, not an every day sight in Las Vegas, were swarming around the block. "I wonder . . ." he trailed off mid-thought.

They quickened their pace. Sure enough, they soon saw just what had been the victim of the blaze.

"Jesus Christ," Amy said. Four stores within the strip mall had been completely burned down. The Information Lounge was one of them, along with a knitting store, a liquor store, and a taco joint.

"Fuck," Ray said. "What happened?"

"I'll find out," Amy answered. She walked up to one of the firemen putting the hose back on his truck. She cocked her hips a bit, put her arms behind her back and arched just a bit. Ray saw her chat with the firefighter a bit, smile, and come back. "Nasty blaze," she reported. "Obviously. They think it started at the internet place, maybe some kind of electrical fire. Nobody got killed, but the internet guy got some second degree burns."

"Jesus," Ray said. "Holy fuck. That's crazy. I was just there. I can't believe that—oh, shit."

"What?" Amy asked.

"What if . . ." Ray took her by the arm and pulled her further from anyone else. They began to walk away quickly. "What if I'm the reason it burned down? That's where I researched the symbol. That fucking symbol. Oh, Jesus. What if this is really big?"

"You think?" Amy asked. "That would be crazy. We should talk to the café guy and see what he knows."

"But we don't know where he is," Ray said.

"Las Vegas Methodist Hospital," Amy said. "The fireman was full of information."

"You're very handy to have around, you know that?" Ray said.

"You have no idea."

# CHAPTER TWENTY-SEVEN

On the bus, Ray and Amy discussed how exactly to get in to see Bill the internet guy. The first plan was to again use Amy's cute factor, but the plan was scrapped upon the realization that most hospital receptionists were women or gay males. They devised a complicated scheme involving Amy's fake pointy ears and an emergency Star Trek fan club meeting, but, in the end, it seemed more of a funny way to ridicule Bill than to actually go in and see him.

It was Amy who thought up the eventual plan. "You've got that detective license. Just show it and say you need to ask him a few questions."

Ray thought about it. He'd never had to use it like that, just as an excuse when cops asked him about why he was taking pictures in a residential area. "What if they don't let me?"

"They will. You're like an authority figure."

"Uh, I guess." Ray wasn't convinced, but Amy seemed to usually be right.

They approached the hospital and Ray stopped. "OK, let me get into character." He stretched his face out. "It was a hot, lonely night in Las Vegas," he said in a deep, gravelly voice. "But things got hotter when SHE walked in."

"What the hell are you doing?" Amy asked, cracking up.

"I'm becoming that kind of private eye. Like Ogami's dad or the ones in the movies. Hard-boiled, instead of hard drinking and hard up. So, come on, baby doll, let's do this thing."

"Rarr," Amy growled.

They entered and walked right up to reception. "May I help you?" Charise at the counter asked.

Ray sidled up to the counter like it was a bar. He took out his license and flashed it. "Ray Brautigan. I'm a detective. Here about the Information      Lounge arson case. Looking for the injured fella. Bill Carter. Burned pretty bad, but not too bad, you know."

"Uhhh, I'm not sure I can—"

Right on cue, Amy cut in. "Oh, please, lady! Mom and dad are on vacation! I've got to go see Billy!"

"And who are you?" Charise asked.

"I'm his sister, Amy. I hired the dick. Something's going on and I need to see my brother!"

"Young miss, even for family—" Charise began. She was interrupted by Amy turning on the tear faucet.

"MY BROTHER! MY BROTHER!" she bawled. "WHY WON'T YOU LET ME SEE MY BROTHER!"

Embarrassment showing through her dark skin, Charise hushed Amy. "Girl! Don't you go throwing a fit on me!" To Ray: "Take her on up to see her brother. Just keep her quiet."

Ray marveled once again at Amy. "Will do, ma'am," he said. "Much obliged."

"He's in room 265B," Charise said.

"Thanks," Ray said. Amy started to walk off, sobbing and Ray leaned back to the counter. "Sorry about her. You know, kids."

"I hear ya there," Charise said. "You see Detective Ramos, tell him Charise says 'Hey.'"

"Will do, ma'am," Ray replied and walked back off before she could press him any further. Amy was waiting for the elevator. "How come you lie so well?" he asked her.

"It's a gift," she said. The smile was a haymaker punch.

The elevator opened and they went on up to the second floor. They followed the signs to 265B. Sure enough, it was Bill the Nerd, arms and legs bandaged up. The room smelled like piss and ointment.

Ray looked at Amy and she gestured for him to go on in. "Bill?" Ray said.

"Huh?" Bill was drugged up fairly well.

"I'm a detective. I'm here to ask you about the fire."

"I already talked to cops. I didn't do it. I told them. I didn't do it." Bill sounded very tired.

"I, uh, I know you didn't, Bill. I believe you. I want to ask you other questions so we can prove you didn't."

"I didn't do it, it was this guy."

"Uh, tell me about this guy," Ray said. Amy took a notepad out of her purse and started writing.

"Big, big guy. Fatter than me." Even under the circumstances Ray had to stifle a chuckle. Still, even an obnoxious nerd didn't deserve this. "Black hair, bushy. Big beard. Really big eyebrows. He was the only person there."

Ray saw Amy jot it down so he didn't pay too much attention, but it sounded kind of familiar. Then again, it wasn't that detailed a description. "Did he do anything, uh, weird or suspicious?" That seemed to be a good question to ask.

"Asked about another customer. But the customer wasn't there so it was weird."

"Who did he ask about?"

"This dumb jackass that smelled like liquor," Bill said, still dazed. "Hey, he looked like you."

Amy faked a coughing fit to mask her laugher.

"Right, yeah," Ray said. "Did you see him do anything?"

"No. Just sat at the computer and looked shit up. I didn't even get to look over his shoulder. He left and after a while all the computers blew up. All those computers. So much money."

"Right," Ray said. "Did you get the guy's name or anything?"

"No. He wrote something down on the sign-in sheet but I didn't look and it's probably burned by now. Do you have any ice cream? I really want some ice cream."

"Uh, I'll talk to a nurse. You've been a big help. We'll, uh, find this guy. Good luck, uh, citizen." Ray grabbed Amy's arm and they headed out.

"I feel kind of bad," he said on the elevator. "He seems really fucked up. And it might be my fault."

"Because you looked up something on his computer?" Amy asked.

"Yeah. I dunno. This seems crazier and crazier. I even think I know what guy he's talking about. O and I saw a fella like that at Jenny's apartment."

"The one with the gun?"

"Yeah."

They left the hospital without another word.

Outside, new cigarettes lit, Amy and Ray walked briskly away from the hospital. "What now?" she asked after a block or two.

"I really don't know. I think I half-expected to be proven wrong by now."

"Should we go to the police?"

"And tell them what?" Ray puffed a deep puff. "Girls avoid me and I think it's because of a symbol, and, oh yeah, this place burned down because of it too? We have nothing."

"Yeah, you're right. I'm not too keen on visiting Bushy Eyebrow Gun Guy right now, if you don't mind."

"Yeah, me neither," Ray said. He stopped on the sidewalk, suddenly aware he was walking nowhere in particular. Down the way you could faintly see the glow of the strip. It was like a UFO had landed a few miles away, in more ways than one.

"Have you tried checking out Cassandra's place?" Amy asked.

"Uh, no. I haven't. I never thought of that."

"Do you know where it is?" That arched brow made him feel stupid and warm at the same time.

"Uh, no."

"You stud! You sleep with a girl and don't even know where she lives!"

Tension broken, Ray laughed again. "Hey, what can I say? They come to me, you know?"

"No, I don't know. So you don't know where she lived. And your internet cafe is now a pile of cinders. I guess we could go to my place to look it up. I've got internet."

"Yeah, OK," Ray said. Then his brain started working again. "Uh, wait. Uh. Um. Don't you, uh, live with, uh, like, your . . .parents?"

"Not really," she said. "They have another place in the suburbs and I stay here to go to school."

"Seriously? Jesus. They let you stay alone? That's crazy."

"I'm seventeen. What, like, in one year I can magically do it but not now? Is there a magic button or a switch? I've tried to find it."

"Uh, I dunno. I just know my folks would have shit their pants if I even asked."

"Guess mine just are less prone to pants crapping."

"Odds are," Ray said. "So how do we get to your place?"

# CHAPTER TWENTY EIGHT

Ray couldn't help but notice that the seventeen year old girl kept a tidier apartment than he did. Amy's place was modestly decorated with an eye for detail. The room was composed well. Nicely-kept band and movie posters. CD collection shelved and probably organized.

"I don't have any bourbon," Amy called from the kitchen. "Scotch OK?"

"Yeah, please, it's great," Ray replied, reading the CD titles. He'd never heard of over three-quarters of the bands. There was a time when he judged people by their taste in music. That was back when he had the time and money to listen to new things.

She brought him a tall glass in the proper style and they clinked again. "Here's to life getting weird. Weirder," Ray said. The Scotch was crisp and clean, with a nice kick at the end. "Mmm. Good."

"I know how to treat my gentleman callers." Nuclear wink.

"So, uh, where's the, uh, computer?" Ray asked, putting a CD back on the shelf.

"My bedroom. Come on," Amy led the way down the short hall. The bedroom was slightly messier than the living room. Clothes were piled up in the corner, probably dirty. Ray did his best not to look at the underwear hanging in various spots. It looked like nice underwear. He tried harder.

"Here, hold on," Amy said. She sat at the computer and fucked with some things that Ray didn't recognize. "I was downloading movies. Don't tell anyone."

"Uh, OK."

"OK, so what's your girlfriend's name again?" Amy asked, ready to type.

"Uh, she's not my girlfriend. It's, uh, Cassandra Reyes."

"She's here in Vegas, right?"

"Yeah," Ray said. "I think she lives on the west side."

"West SIIIIDE!" Amy flashed her best gang sign. It was a bit better than it should be. "A Crip taught me that."

"You, uh, you know a Crip?"

Amy smiled the smile that showed why a Crip would teach her something. "Yeah. He dropped out of my school. He's sweet, but pretty stupid."

Ray wondered how often she thought that of people. "Sweet but stupid." Was he one of them? Ray wasn't sure which half of the description was worse. "Sweet" meant "unfuckable loser" and "stupid" meant, well, stupid. The more he thought of it, the more he realized that, yeah, that was him. And then he remembered Amy's age and stared intently at the floor.

"Mmmmkay," Amy said. "Got a couple of possibilities here. You said the west side, though, right?"

"Yeah, I'm pretty sure."

"OK. Well, that eliminates this one. So does 89 *del Fuego* Lane sound about right?"

Ray had no idea. "I have no idea. I guess."

Amy looked at her watch. "Hm. A little late to be exploring strange neighborhoods. We should probably crash for the night."

"Shit. You have school tomorrow. I keep forgetting I have a friend who has to go to school." Ray said, not looking at the red lacy bra on the closet door.

"I could skip, if you want. No tests or anything tomorrow."

"Oh, God," Ray said. "I can't ask you to do that. That's crazy. I'm a horrible influence. We're drinking, I'm old, it's a school night, I got you wrapped up in this—"

"Ray, shut it," Amy said. "I'd be out this late anyway, and it's not like I never saw booze before you."

"Uh, yeah, I guess you're right. Just feel kind of, you know, guilty."

"Yeah, I noticed," Amy said. "You've been staring at the floor for a while. Sorry this room's a mess. You don't want to see all my stuff lying around."

"Uh, it's OK," Ray said, looking up momentarily. "I should, uh, go now."

"You're pretty far from home. You should crash here."

Ray's face lit up like a fake fireplace in a white trash one bedroom. "Uh, ur, uh."

"Christ, Ray. If I promise not to molest you in your sleep would you chill the fuck out?"

"Uh, um," Ray stammered again. "I know, I just, you, you're so young, and—shit, I'm sorry, Amy. I just, uh, it freaked me out. You're sure your parents won't come in and see me and be all crazy?"

"I'm sure, Ray. If it makes you feel better, you can take the couch or the floor here or something." Ray tried to remember the couch but was certain it must be more comfortable than his futon, which he still hadn't replaced. Then he wondered how he could possibly be even considering staying at a seventeen-year-old's apartment.

"I dunno, I—"

"Ray! Do I have to take the no-molesting promise? Do I?"

"Uh, no," he said finally. She was calming him down, which was a difficult task at this point. He tried to rationalize it. It would take so long to get home, and he didn't even know where his bus connection would be. And that couch would be comfortable as hell. The bed would be more comfortable. No, no, the couch. The bed was a bad idea. Would she even let him? No. Bad idea. Not worth considering. "Uh, OK. Yeah. I'll, uh, I'll stay on the, uh, couch."

"I'll miss ya!" she said and Ray wondered what she meant. She got ready for bed quickly and Ray couldn't stop wondering what the hell he was doing. He lied down on the couch and, yeah, it was really comfortable. Nice and fluffy, the kind you nap on after big turkey dinners. He would get very comfortable, cozy, even, but a stray thought would distract the hell out of him. The thought usually involved Amy, but occasionally Jenny or Cass.

Amy was close, though, and she'd occasionally go from the bathroom to her room in a t-shirt and boxers. *'Jesus Christ in heaven,'* Ray half-prayed. Her legs were strong and smooth, and her ass was—something he was not going to think about.

She turned off his light and wished him good night. He returned it. "Need me to tuck you in?" she asked, giggling.

"Uh," he said. *'Yes,'* he thought. "No," he said.

"OK. Well, sleep tight, but with one eye open. I never made that anti-molestation pledge."

Sleep came with great difficulty for Ray Brautigan that night.

# CHAPTER TWENTY-NINE

And morning came like a gunshot at a picnic: unwelcome, loud, and shocking.

"Gah! Fuck!" Ray screamed, sitting straight up. He oriented himself, remembering where he had spent the night. He felt a morning hard-on hitting his pants and crossed his legs. Amy was running around the apartment getting ready. Her TV was blaring. This was probably what scared the shit out of him.

"Hey, sorry!" Amy said. "Kind of forgot you were here. I'll turn it down."

"No, no s'okay," Ray said, wishing he could stand up and go to the bathroom. Instead, things got worse as Amy plopped down next to him on the couch, brushing her teeth.

"You schleep OK?"

Ray nodded. "Yeah, fine."

"Good. You didn't feel me molescht you?" A bit of toothpaste flew onto Ray's face as she laughed.

"Uh, heh, um."

Amy reached up and wiped his face with a long, thin finger. "Schorry." She got up to go spit in the bathroom. Ray's boner was worse than before. He heard her rinse her mouth out and she came out, ready for, well, school.

"I've gotta run, Ray," she said. "If you find out anything, call me and leave a message. I'll call you after school and we'll meet back up. Don't do anything stupid."

"Uh, OK," he said.

She stood over him for a second. "Hello! I'm leaving! Stand up for Christ's sake! God, what happened to chivalry?"

"Uh, ur," Ray said, getting up, hoping his hard-on would magically fade away.

She grabbed him and hugged him tight. He, unable to resist, put his arms around her but tried to back his crotch away.

"What's wrong with you?"

"Uh, nothing," Ray said. She didn't let go. She hugged him tighter, in fact.

"Oh, hello!" she said. "That's nothing to be ashamed of, not at all. Good morning to you, too!" Ray found new levels of red. She kissed him on the cheek softly and he, after a moment's hesitation, returned it. They held each other a second longer before parting.

"Thanks for, uh, letting me, uh, stay here," Ray said, missing the embrace's warmth, but still embarrassed by his dick's behavior.

"No problem. We'll have to do it again sometime. That is, if all your other girlfriends let you. The door locks automatically. Have some breakfast and chill here a while if you want. Cassandra's address is still on my screen."

"Wow. Cool, thanks," Ray said.

They hugged again. "Bye," Amy said. They cheek-kissed again. And then she left. Ray ran to the bathroom and impatiently waited for his dick to go limp enough that he could pee without ruining Amy's bathroom.

He later walked around the apartment fighting several temptations. He decided to check her fridge and actually poured himself a bowl of cereal. It had sugary marshmallows and was real good. He hadn't had it in years, and knew that it probably wasn't going to agree with him. But it all seemed worthwhile in that nice little eat-in kitchen on an early morning. It was like the cool parts of waking up next to someone, without all the shame of drunken bad sex.

He knew it couldn't last, though. As much as he wanted to just stay at Amy's place, he had work to do. Cassandra's place needed to be checked out. He called her phone one more time to no avail. Either she was in on something or she was in trouble, too. Whichever it was, he wanted to find her. What he'd do then, he had no idea.

He went to Amy's bedroom and tried to focus on the computer screen again. He jotted down the address. '89 del Fuego *Lane, Apartment 3A. Front of the building, probably, then.*' His zoom lens would probably actually be able to see in the place, but he had never snooped in broad daylight before. And he didn't particularly feel like waiting all day.

Then his phone rang, startling him. He answered, "Brautigan."

"Hey, you're actually up! Holy shit!" It was Ogami. "When's the last time you saw the light of day?"

"I could ask you the same thing. What's going on?"

"Hey, I got your message, man. What the fuck's going on?"

"Shit, long story. What are you doing? Can you pick me up?"

"Soph had an early morning, so I'm up with nothing to do. Where are you, home?"

"Uh, no," Ray said. He told Ogami to pick him up at Amy's address, artfully leaving out the fact that it was Amy's address.

"Ray, dude, this better be a good story," Ogami said. "See you in a bit."

Ray finished his sugary breakfast and remembered to rinse out his cereal bowl. This was a place to keep neat. He stepped outside, smoked a cigarette, and waited. He liked being outside. A lot less temptation to snoop around or touch things he ought not to touch. It would be good to have Ogami around. Since the last time they'd spoken, enough had happened that Ogami would be just as suspicious as Ray. And it never feels good for a best friend to think you're nuts.

And if Ray was jumped the other night not in some random act, but because of all this, it wouldn't hurt to have a 6'3" professional baseball player with a short temper. Ogami's mere presence had often gotten Ray out of well-deserved ass-kickings. Ray hoped it would also work for undeserved ones.

# CHAPTER THIRTY

"Nice looking place," Ogami said as they pulled out of the driveway. "Whose is it?"

Ray bit the bullet. "Amy's."

"Amy the hot teenager Amy?"

"Yes." Ray looked out the window.

"Holy shit! Did you get laid two nights in a row with different girls? Did you? Holy shit!" Ogami turned the stereo down for this.

"No, no, no. I just crashed there. We were actually — there's something going on. Something bad, O. Remember when I was worried about Jenny and that symbol? I was right to be worried."

"Why?" Ogami asked, and Ray explained. As the story went on, Ogami pulled into a strip mall parking lot to concentrate on it.

"And now I want to check out Cass' place. Well, we think it's her place. I want to see if I can find anything. Uh, a clue, or something, I guess."

"Shit. You're a real detective now," Ogami said. "This shit is crazy. Sorry I talked you out of believing anything."

"No, you were right. It was crazy. It IS crazy. But, now, you know, I . . .I have to know. Something's going on and it affected Jenny and I have to know."

"OK," Ogami said, taking the car out of park. "So where we off to now?"

"Uh, 89 *del Fuego* Lane," Ray replied. "Here's hoping it isn't burned down."

It wasn't. It didn't take too long to get there. The neighborhood was better than Ray's, but not by much. There was less litter, but the buildings didn't look to be much better off. Cassandra's building was a four story boxy building without any kind of architectural character. Nobody put any thought into the design of the parts of Vegas not meant to suck in tourists. They're just utilitarian places to sleep in between service shifts.

Ogami parallel-parked across the street and they looked at the building. Ray looked up to the third floor and couldn't really see anything. Curtains were drawn. Even with his camera, it wouldn't have been much.

"What now?" Ogami asked.

"Uh, I don't really know," Ray said. "I, uh, could go look at the building, maybe?"

"What's that going to do?"

"I don't know. Maybe if I buzz someone will let me in?"

"Then what?"

Ray sat and thought. "Shit," he said. "I figured the next thing to do would be obvious. Maybe we should call your dad. He could — oh, shit!"

"What?" Ogami asked.

"Fuck, man! That dude! Look, with Cass!" Ray pointed towards the building at a man and woman leaving the building. They both carried what looked to be full duffel bags.

"Where do I recognize him from? He's fucking familiar as shit," Ogami said.

"He's the fucker with the gun from Saturday!"

"Fuck! You're right!"

"Are they leaving together or is he making her go?" Ray asked, squinting for detail.

"I don't know. I can't tell."

The fat man and Cass got into a car.

"Should I follow them?" Ogami asked.

"Huh? Fuck. Follow them? Shit! I don't know."

The car with Cass in it pulled out and started driving.

"Shit," Ray continued. "Uh, yeah. Yeah, follow them. Fuck."

Ogami started the car and coasted down the road after them. "Holy shit, Ray! We're having a car chase! This is awesome! Much better than following Amy's gay boyfriend! This is, like, real!"

"We're going, like, fifteen miles per hour in a residential zone."

"I know, but still! Wait, what if he pulls a piece? What then?"

"Why the hell would he do that? He probably wouldn't even consider someone's following him. I can't believe WE considered it!"

"Hey, maybe you should duck down, just in case," Ogami said. "Like, either one of them could recognize you."

"Shit," Ray said, hunching down. "You're right. But what if he's kidnapping Cass? Then maybe she SHOULD see me."

"I think we should err on the side of caution, Ray. That guy pointed a gun at me. I don't like having guns pointed at me very much."

"Good point," Ray said, back already cramping. "Shit, what's going on?" The car jerked around a corner.

"They're uh, they're speeding up. Should we follow them? FUCK! They're really going!" Without waiting for an answer, Ogami revved up his engine and took off after them.

"Ahh! Fuck!" Ray yelled as his head bounced off the dashboard from the jerk. "Jesus Christ! Slow down!"

"No, man, I can't!" Ogami was staring out the windshield. "I'll lose them! Fuck!"

"But, but," Ray sat up enough to look at the speedometer, "we're speeding, man!"

"I think they know we're following them!" Ogami shouted.

"Either that or they drive like this all the time! Fuck! Shit!" Ever since a car accident when he was eighteen, Ray hated going fast in an automobile. He sat up straight, with knuckles whiter than a starlet's teeth. "SLOW DOWN!"

At that moment, the loud blurt of a police siren scared both men shitless. "Oh, fuck," Ogami said, sensing a disappointing end to the adrenaline rush. "What should I do?"

"Uh, pull over! Fuck, a cop! I'm sorry, man."

"Don't sweat it," Ogami said, slowing down and pulling over. "My record's clean. What do we say?"

"Um, fuck. I don't know."

"Quick, Ray," Ogami insisted. "Do we tell them or not?"

"Fuck. I don't think so. It's, uh, it's kind of crazy and shit. We don't have any proof." By this time the officer had walked up to Ogami's window and knocked on it. Ogami rolled it down.

"Uh, hello, sir," Ogami said.

"License and registration, Andretti."

"Uh, yes, sir." Ogami had a huge rebellious streak, but his folks had always taught him that pissing off a police officer is very, very rarely a good idea, especially in Las Vegas. Ray nervously tried to find something to look at as the officer looked at Ogami's papers.

"Doin' quite a clip back there, boys. Any good reason?"

"Uh, no, sir. We were, uh, following a friend and they, uh, well, they lost us, sir. It was really, uh, quite stupid."

The officer silently read for a moment or two. "You the Ogami who plays for the Rollers?"

"Uh, yes, sir," Ogami said with obvious hope. Ray realized this might actually work out OK.

"You'd be a decent player if you could keep your ass in the game."

"Uh, thank you, sir," Ogami replied, unsure of pretty much everything at this point.

"Here's the deal, Burroughs. I'm letting you off with a warning. You get your ass thrown out of one more game, and I will find you, and you will be fined for something. Something big. You understand me? Are we goddam crystal goddam clear?"

"Yes sir, we are," Ogami replied. The battle between intellect and pride is a rough one. Nine times out of ten, pride kicks intellect in the balls for a cheap win. But every now and then, intellect remembers it's smarter, tricks pride, and then kicks it in the balls. Ogami's pride wanted to puke as the officer went back to his car.

"Jesus Christ," Ray said.

"God. That was scary shit. Why are cops so goddam scary? It's not like we're in LA or something. Jesus."

They sat there for a moment and watch the officer pull away. "What now?" Ogami finally asked.

"I dunno," Ray replied. "Maybe that guy went back to Jenny's place. We could, uh, I dunno, go there?"

"Dude's got a gun," Ogami said. "We don't have a gun. Wait, do we?"

"No!" Ray yelped. "Why the fuck would we have a gun?"

"Because you're a private investigator?"

"Har har," Ray said. "Did your dad have one?"

"Yeah, I think so. But then, his 'investigations' weren't old fatties cheating on other old fatties."

"Point, point," Ray said, lighting a cigarette. "Jesus." He exhaled loudly and tried to relax some. "Let's go to my place. I want to get my camera. I need something, at least."

"On our way, Green Hornet," Ogami said as they pulled back into the street.

# CHAPTER THIRTY-ONE

Ogami looked around as Ray packed up all his photography equipment. "Hey, you cleaned," he said. "I didn't know you had hardwood floors." Ray flipped him the bird in reply.

"Here we go," Ray said, fastening his camera bag. "Telephoto, some filters for night vision if we need it, and lots of film. If I get enough photos that show something fucked up is going on, then maybe we can take it to the cops."

Ray's phone began to ring. "Brautigan," he said.

"Hey, dork, it's Amy."

"Oh. Amy! Hi."

Ogami immediately began making kissy faces.

"What's going on?" she said.

"We, uh, Ogami and I went to Cass' place. We saw the big guy that pulled a gun on me and that probably torched the Information Lounge. He and Cass got in his van and drove off, but they lost us. I think we're going to Jenny's place now."

"Wow. Uh, I'm not out of school for another hour, you want me to skip out?"

While Ogami made humping motions in the air, Ray replied, "No. I've got my telephoto so I'll just stay back. Shouldn't be a problem." Ray was trying hard as hell not to laugh. It occurred to him that he was about to risk great harm potentially, but he was talking on the phone with a girl in high school and laughing at his best friend. He was almost having fun, except for the possible injury and death business.

"OK, then. I'll call you later. Take care of yourself, stud."

"Bye, Amy."

"You looooove her!" Ogami sang. "You want to maaaaaarry her!" Why did everyone in Ray's life love this routine?

"Shut up, O!" The two men smiled in spite of their situation. "So. Let's go do something really stupid."

"Sounds like a plan," Ogami said as they left Ray's apartment. They drove towards Jenny's neighborhood but made sure not to get close. Ray figured that Ogami's car was pretty memorable, and that since Fat Gun Guy had probably seen them following him, it wouldn't be that great an idea to pull up to the place.

"You stay in the car, in case we have to get the fuck out of here," Ray said. "I'm gonna go hide and snap some photos."

"Is that a good idea? Won't they see you?"

"It's my job, O. I do this all the time. It's easier to hide from people than you'd think. Nobody really looks too hard when they're home."

Ray attached his telephoto lens, the most powerful he had. He got out of the car and told Ogami, "If I, uh, get into trouble or something, I'll, uh, I'll scream 'OH FUCK' really loud."

"Helluva code word," Ogami said. "Go see what's going on, man. Watch your back."

Ray closed the car door and looked down the block. After a few years of dicking, he'd gotten pretty good at finding inconspicuous places to hide and take photos. There was a fire escape across the street, but that would be noisy. A bunch of garbage cans, but the angle would be not so good. He settled on an alleyway in between two apartment buildings where he'd be shaded enough not to be seen from Jenny's loft.

Ray casually walked into the area and took out his camera. The two apartment buildings he was between had no windows near him, so he was safe. Anyone gave him shit about doing photos, he'd just give them a line about a college class. That worked frighteningly well in most cases. People don't question that excuse enough.

He steadied the camera and began looking through the windows. The first one showed nothing, just curtains. He moved to the left and saw . . .just a room, nothing. Slowly, fearfully, he moved on to Jenny's window. There was someone in there. He adjusted his focus. It was a woman. Ray fumbled and almost dropped his camera out of nervousness. He tried looking through the camera again but he fell down as something big and hard hit his head. He tried to scream but a kick in the gut knocked the wind out of him. He wanted to look at his assailant this time, but another kick to his face sent blood into his eyes

"You stupid fuck, you don't belong here. Gonna fuckin get you now," Ray heard as the world swirled around him. He tried screaming again when he got his breath back, but he choked on what was probably blood, maybe vomit, or, actually, most likely both. He let out a large grunt instead. Then something hit him in the stomach again. He heard something click, and though he'd not heard that sound in real life much, he immediately recognized it as a gun.

"FUCK!" he screamed.

"Stupid dick," the other man said. "Nobody gonna answer you in this spic town. Go fuck yoursuuunnhhhf," the man's voice got funny right after there was a loud crack.

'Oh, fuck, I'm dying,' Ray thought. 'I'm dying and I don't know if she's OK. I love her.'

"Ray?" he heard. "Ray, shit, man, are you OK? Talk to me Ray." Something wiped his face and the blood from his eyes. Ray looked up and saw Ogami crouching over him. "Ray, can you hear me?"

"Yeah," Ray replied. "Oh fuck I hurt. What the fuck? That fuck had a fucking gun I think. Did he fucking shoot me? Why are you here? Fuck?" Ray kept talking and talking and wasn't sure what he was saying.

"Ray, dude, shut up." That seemed to be a good idea so Ray followed Ogami's advice. He sat up slowly and felt around his body for anything that might be broken or sticking out. He was extremely sore but everything seemed to generally be in the right place.

"Fuck. I really got my ass kicked, man. What happened?"

"Well, I heard you say 'Unnnnh fuck' and I figured that was close enough to 'Oh fuck' and I came running. I saw this motherfucker about to fucking shoot you so I popped him." At this point, Ogami held up his practice bat, a nice heavy Louisville Slugger. Ray looked around his friend and saw his assailant lying face down on the ground in a crumpled heap.

"Holy shit," Ray said.

"Yeah, I know. You have no idea how long I've had the desire to fucking clock somebody with a bat. There's never really a good time to do it. Well, except this, I guess."

"Where's his gun?" Ray asked, struggling to stand up. Ogami turned around and pointed to the pistol stuck in the back of his pants.

"I should take this out. I don't know if the safety's on or anything." Ogami carefully took the gun out of his pants, adrenaline finally wearing off again. "Oh, Jesus. He's not moving. Did I kill him?"

Ray walked to the man and flipped him over. It was the same big guy with the bushy eyebrows that had taken Cass. He put his head near his heart and heard it pumping. "No, he's alive." Ray stood back up and looked at him. "Fucking asshole. Motherfucking asshole. Goddam POINT A GUN AT ME?!?" Ray began screaming. He kicked the prone man in his large stomach. "YOU LIKE IT? HOW DO YOU LIKE IT?" Another kick to his head. A stomp. And then Ogami grabbed Ray and drug him backwards.

"Jesus, bud, settle down." Ray was breathing hard and could hear his heart in his ears. He didn't struggle against Ogami, though. He knew O was right.

"Fuck," he said. "Sorry."

"It's OK. It wasn't me you were kicking," O said. "So what the fuck do we do now?"

"Jesus. I don't know. I guess we could call the cops or something. He pulled a gun on me and beat me up. That's illegal, it has to be."

"Yeah. And did you see anything else?"

Ray looked around for his camera. "Almost. Hold on." He picked it up off the ground. The lens was a bit scratched, but thankfully it was pretty much OK. "Let me . . .shit," Ray said as he saw more clearly into Jenny's room. There was a fight going on, some kind of struggle. "Shit shit shit!"

"What?" Ogami asked. "What the fuck's going on?"

"Somebody's getting beat to shit in there, I think. There's something—something bad. Shit. Shit. What do we do?"

"Uh, call the cops still?"

"It's right now! Fuck! I don't know if we should wait. Fuck!" Ray zoomed and focused as much as he could but it was too far away and there was too much glare to get a better view.

"Well, then, shut the fuck up and let's go break in there."

Ogami took off, bat still in hand.

"Wait! Fuck. Shit! Ogami! Goddammit!" Ray watched his friend run towards Jenny's loft. "Oh God damn it," he said.

# CHAPTER THIRTY-TWO

"We'll need these," Ray said to a huffing and puffing Ogami. Ogami looked at his friend who was holding a set of keys he'd taken off his assailant.

"Oh. Yeah. Do you have that gun?"

"Yes. Fuck. Yes. I have a goddam gun. Oh, Jesus. What are we doing? We should go."

"What if they're hurting Cassandra? What if they're hurting Jenny?"

Ray swallowed and realized that now was no time to leave a friend behind. He tried a few of the keys and finally got one to work. He opened the door and just kind of stared inside. "This is fucking crazy," he whispered.

"You should take the gun out maybe," Ogami said, bat still in hand.

"Oh, Jesus," Ray said, taking it out of his pocket. He had held a gun once when he was eight when his uncle took him to a firing range for no apparent reason. It scared the shit out of him then so bad that he couldn't play with his GI Joes for a month.

His hands started shaking so bad he felt he was going to drop the gun. "Maybe you should hold the gun," he whispered.

"But you're no good with a bat," Ogami protested quietly.

"That doesn't make any sense," Ray said.

"Shut up and go! We can't waste time arguing." Ogami was right about that, so Ray started creeping up the stairs. If he opened the door with the keys calmly enough whoever else was inside probably would just assume he was Bushybeard. But how was he going to do that while still holding that goddam scary ass gun? He handed the keys to Ogami.

"You'll have to open the door then. I can't open it with this goddam gun in my hands."

Ogami nodded and took the keys. They ascended the three flights, trying to time their steps so they didn't sound like two people. As they got further up, they could hear a commotion, some things banging around and shouting. These fuckers were lucky; the neighborhood heard this kind of shit all the time. Nobody called the cops. You just didn't do that.

It's why Jenny had always had the best parties. You could fuck shit up all hours of the night and no idiot neighbor was going to complain. Hell, they were probably blasting their own music anyway.

Ray remembered one party, packed to the gills with people he didn't know. He was drinking at a table with Jenny. She pointed to an attractive girl in some crazy 40s get-up. "We could probably take her to your place tonight," Jenny had said. Ray had laughed nervously, not sure what to say, if she was joking, if it was a good idea . . .he panicked inside and said nothing. Nothing happened.

From time to time he thought about that night. And at this point he thought of it again, right outside Jenny's door. He and Ogami locked eyes. They paused for a moment. Ray had to piss and shit and throw up at the same time. He was fairly sure it was going to happen whether he let it or not. Also, a heart attack. A pants-shitting heart attack.

He jumped as he heard a woman scream and that was it. He nodded at Ogami, who opened the door. Well, he tried. The first key wasn't right. Ray got scared and raised the gun, just in case. Second key, no go.

"Fuck," Ogami said quietly. He stuck a third key in and nearly dropped the entire set. "Jesus, I think I'm fucking nervous!" He put the third key back in and it fit. He turned the lock and opened the door.

Ray immediately raised the gun and tried to swing it around like on the cop shows, but no one was in the entrance hallway. Ogami followed in and quickly shut the door. The ruckus was coming from Jenny's old room.

"Tyler, that you?" a nasally male voice called out.

Ray quickly looked at Ogami, who did likewise.

"Come in here, this one isn't cooperating," the nasal man said.

Ogami started walking towards the door quietly, so Ray went as well. He couldn't keep his hand steady. They got near the door and Ogami motioned for him to go in. Ray wondered why HE had to go in, but it was probably because he had the goddam gun.

Then he heard the nasal voice again. "I'm gonna give you one more chance. Tell us what you know or Tyler shoots you in the goddam stomach, bitch."

"Fuck you," a female voice said, exhausted. "I don't know what you're talking about." Ray almost didn't recognize it. He'd never heard Jenny so tired, so devoid of life. She sounded awful.

He jumped in the room, gun in front. "FUCK YOU, YOU FUCKING FUCK! FUCKING LET HER FUCKING GO!"

The man turned around. He was of average build, but his arms seemed a little short for his body. His forehead was high and his hair kept short. He wore a plain t-shirt and khakis. Both had a bit of blood on them. He stared at the gun coldly.

Jenny was behind him, tied to a chair. She'd been hit around. Quite a bit. Ray's face went hot and throbbing. "RAY?!?" she said incredulously.

"I knew you knew something," the man said. "This must be a compatriot of yours. Come to rescue your comrade?"

"Fuck you talkin about?" Ray asked.

"Whatever. God, this 'playing dumb' thing gets tedious. I wish you people would just admit it."

Ray tried to figure out what that meant but realized it wasn't important. "Untie her," he said. "Or I'll shoot you and make you die."

"Very well," he said.

"Orf!" Ogami called out. Ray spun around to see what was going on. Ogami had been tackled by Michael, the guy who had let them in that last time they came here. Ray tried to aim the gun but he felt something hit his head and the burning started again. He felt the gun fall away and he scrabbled to pick it back up.

Ogami knocked Michael off him and was facing him off with the bat. Ray scrambled towards the gun, but the other man beat him to it.

"Tell the Natural over there to put Wonderbat down," he said.

"O," Ray said. Ogami looked around and saw the situation. He put the bat down.

"You fucking turned your back on me?" the man said. "Maybe you really aren't working for the government."

"I really have no idea what's going on. I just came to help my friend," Ray said. The gun was pointed at him. He wanted a drink very, very, very badly. "Oh, Jesus."

"You don't even know how to use a gun, do you?" nasal guy said. Ray shook his head.

"Ray, oh, Ray. Oh, Jesus," Jenny said. "Why did you . . .how in hell did you . . .what the fuck are you doing?"

"Rescuing you," Ogami piped in.

"These men are not agents. My God. You really didn't know anything, did you?" the man turned and asked Jenny.

"No. I've been trying to tell you that."

"Where's Cassandra?" Ray heard himself ask.

"She'll be dealt with soon enough," Michael replied.

"You people are pathetic," the other man said. "You really don't know shit and here you are and now we have to fucking kill you all. Jesus. Nice luck, assholes."

"Yeah, I know," Ray said. "Par for the fucking course." It was over now, and Ray knew it. He almost didn't give a shit anymore. He felt tingly and numb. It really didn't matter. There Jenny was. She wasn't smiling that smile that he'd always liked, but there she was. He'd failed her, but at least he got to see her.

"Jenny," he said. "Jenny. I . . .I just wanted . . .I'm sorry I didn't come earlier." Ray had lost all control of his tongue. Meaning and words flew out like water from a fire hydrant in the ghetto. "You . . .you, you mean a lot to me. I, uh, I have very strong feelings . . .I, uh, I think I—"

"Oh, do shut up," the apparent leader of the men said, raising his gun straight to Ray's head.

Ray felt his body grow warm and he felt something run down the back of his leg, soft and hot.

"Did you just shit your pants?" Jenny asked.

"Michael, get Cassandra. If she wants to prove we can trust her, she'll do it."

"OK, Stephen," Michael said, then left the room and quickly returned with Cassandra. At least now Ray knew the name of the fucker behind this.

"Ray?!?" she said. "Oh, God. No. I didn't want you to get involved in this."

"What the fuck IS this?!?" Ray asked.

"Oh, God," Cassandra replied.

"You KNOW her?" Jenny asked.

"Shut up," Stephen said. "Cassandra, you'll eliminate them. You fucked up and brought this fucker right to us. You pull the trigger.

"Stephen! Shit! Can't you just . . .make them promise not to tell? They don't know anything!"

"First you want to join us," Stephen said. "Then you don't have the stomach for real revolution. Then you 'accidentally' get wrapped up in these people and now you want them to live? You're a dilettante, Cassandra. Here is your option: either they die alone, or you die with them. Decide now. Michael, give her your gun."

"But—" Michael stammered.

"Now," Stephen said with emphasis.

"Oh, fuck," Ogami said.

Cassandra's face twisted with emotion. "Goddammit, I just—" Cassandra looked at Ray. "I'm sorry, Ray." She held her hand out for Michael's gun. He took it out of the back of his pants and gave it to her. Then he went back to the door to prevent, it seemed, anyone from escaping.

"Fuck. Cass! No, oh, God, no. I don't even know what's going on. Let Jenny go."

Cassandra stepped towards Ray and aimed the gun at his head. "I'm sorry about all this, I really am. If it helps anything, I really did like you."

As Ray was about to emit fluids from every orifice he had, she quickly turned around and pulled the trigger at Stephen. There was the snap of an empty gun. "Shit," she said. Stephen aimed his own pistol at Cass casually.

"What kind of fucking moron do you take me for, Cass? You wouldn't even fuck me and I was your leader! You're not going to shoot this piece of shit! Like we'd trust a level one like Michael with a loaded firearm . . ."

Ray heard several loud noises all happen at once. There was a gunshot, a woman's scream, and a man's scream. He looked at Jenny, she was OK. Cassandra was on the ground, bleeding, but her eyes were open. Michael, near the door, wasn't moving.

Everyone turned towards the fallen hump in surprise. Walking past him was a short, fat man with a bloody knife in one hand and a pistol in the other. It was Frankie. The pistol was leveled at Stephen and it was a goddam big one. "You will be putting away your firearm now, fucker," Frankie said.

"Frankie?" Ray said, still trying to put it all together.

"I put tail on you when you get mugged. I do not like my friends being hurt. I do not like the money I pay being stolen. I do not like stupid motherfuckers pulling goddam horseshit in my America. I do not like stupid fucks who have not put their fucking guns on the fucking floor yet. I want to kill them."

Stephen seemed to consider things for a moment. After that moment, the decision he made must have been "put the gun down and live." He set the gun down gently and kicked it towards Frankie.

"I have other people here," Stephen said, still frightened.

"They are dead," Frankie said. "My nephew and I made them go quiet. Ray my boy, untie your girlfriend."

"She's not—" Ray started, but decided that untying her was the proper response no matter who she was to him.

"Now," Frankie went on. "Question is, who wants to stay here as I shove my knife in this motherfucker's dick hole and show him what torture is back in home lands?"

"Uhh," Ray said, ineptly fiddling with the knots. Ogami seemed to consider it for a moment.

"I'd love to, guys, but, I think I need some medical attention," Cass called from the floor.

"Oh, shit! Cass!" Ray said. "Anyone have a phone that works?"

"Do not worry, Ray my boy. I have called a detective friend of mine who enjoys pictures of things in assholes. Things are arranged, as they say. You take beautiful women to hospital, Frankie will clean things up here. I hear ambulance now."

"Seriously, you can—"

"Ray, my boy. Shut the fuck up, if you do not mind my saying. You all need to see a doctor to fix you. And someone is needing a new pair of pants."

Things got fuzzy at that point, either from the shock or the passing out, but there was definitely an ambulance involved.

# CHAPTER THIRTY-THREE

Ray woke up in a hospital bed, off-white sterility surrounding him. Everything hurt.

"Oh Jesus fuck," he sort of said. His voice wasn't so good. He recognized the pain as being from stomach acids in vomit having burned him a bit. Here he was, waking up alone in a hospital again. He wondered if this really was the first time, actually, if the whole insane past few days were just some kind of fever dream. "I need a fucking drink," he said to all the Off-White.

"Ray?" the wall answered back. No, the doorway. No, Ogami. "Ray, you awake?"

"Yes ouch. Everything hurts. I need booze."

Ogami came up to Ray's bed. He reached into his back pocket and pulled out a plastic flask. "Never leave home without an emergency flask," he said. He handed it over to Ray who drank a big gulp thankfully.

"Oh, fuck, that's good," he said. "Oh, fuck. Shit. What happened? Oh, fuck. I feel funny."

"You passed out you giant pussy. They got you doped up, too, lucky. Said you were in shock."

"Fuck," Ray said and it felt like verbal molasses. "We had fucking guns pointed as us! People got shot! People got fucking killed! Frankie— "

"Shhh!" Ogami hushed him. "Shut up, dumbass."

"Oh," Ray said, head sloshing like it was three a.m. at the Hole.

"Look who's here," Ogami said, pointing at the door. Ray squinted and saw something shapely that came towards him.

"I leave you alone for a few hours and you end up in the hospital," Amy said. "I need a leash for you or something."

"Amy?" Ray asked.

"Yeah. That must be some good shit they've got you on there. I heard about the guns and all that crazy stuff. Jesus. I heard you shat your pants."

Ray blushed hard despite his haze. "That blush never gets old," Amy said. She leaned over and kissed him on the cheek. He was pretty sure he didn't look down her shirt.

Memories flashed again. "Jesus. They were going to kill us, O. Fuck. Fuck. They were going to kill us. They shot Cass!"

"She's in intensive care," Amy said. "She's serious but she'll be OK, they said. She's hot. Lucky!"

"Oh, good, that's good." Every word felt like it oozed off Ray's tongue. It occurred to him that he'd probably really enjoy these drugs under other circumstances. Then he remembered. "Jenny! Where's Jenny?"

"Trying to sleep, you loud retard!" Confused, Ray sloshed his head around again, and saw Jenny poking her head out from the room-divider curtain. "God, don't you ever shut up?"

"I'm on drugs, Jenny!" Ray said for some reason.

She laughed. "Yeah, me, too. I guess this is the upside of being tortured. Fuck! I was fucking tortured!"

"Did they . . .uh, did they . . ." Ray started.

"Huh? Oh. No. They just hit me around. I guess that's torture. I mean, it's no Torquemada or anything, but I sure didn't expect that when I left the house."

"Three months and — "

"Three months? No, they just got me a few days ago," Jenny said.

"Oh," Ray said.

"Hey, I was, uh, on my way to getting a soda. You guys OK?" Ogami asked.

Ray nodded and Ogami left the room, taking Amy with him.

"Ray," Jenny said. "Thanks. Thanks for sticking with me. And, uh, rescuing me. From that guy who was torturing me."

"You're welcome," Ray said. He thought a lot of other things. The thoughts screamed in his muddled head, but he didn't say them. He thought that, maybe, in spite of his stupor, his face said them all anyway. And saying them out loud would only result in Jenny making fun of him. "You're my friend and I love you," Ray said anyway, just as he had decided not to.

"BARF!" Jenny teased. "God, you big sissy. You are such a loser. At least this time you didn't shit yourself." But she smiled that smile at him. It was bruised and it was tattered, but there it was, that smile. Ray leaned back and wondered if anyone had bothered to wash his ass.

Printed in the United States
52021LVS00003B/79-81